'Crisis toda turned his kettle.

He was wearing his boxer shorts and nothing else. That was what he always wore while he ate breakfast, and why his lack of clothes bothered him now he didn't know.

'What precautions are we taking?' Rachel asked, waiting for him to finish at the sink so she could pour bowls of water for the dogs. Then she turned her attention to toast, as though she was completely unaware of him.

How could she be unaware of him? he thought savagely. He was climbing walls here! Seeing her in her shorts and her tiny crop top, that left nothing to the imagination, he was so aware of her that everything else was blotted out completely.

Like the little matter of a town threatened by bushfire.

Marion Lennox was born on an Australian dairy farm. She moved on—mostly because the cows weren't interested in her stories! Marion writes Medical Romance™ as well as Tender Romance™. Initially she used different names, so if you're looking for past books, search also for author Trisha David. In her non-writing life Marion cares (haphazardly) for her husband, teenagers, dogs, cats, chickens and anyone else who lines up at her dinner table. She fights her rampant garden (she's losing) and her house dust (she's lost). She also travels, which she finds seriously addictive. As a teenager Marion was told she'd never get anywhere reading romance. Now romance is the basis of her stories, her stories allow her to travel, and if ever there was an advertisement for following your dream, she'd be it! You can contact Marion at www.marionlennox.com

Recent titles by the same author:

IN DR DARLING'S CARE
 (Medical Romance™)
HER ROYAL BABY
 (Tender Romance™)
STORMBOUND SURGEON
 (Medical Romance™)
TO THE DOCTOR: A DAUGHTER
 (Medical Romance™)
A MILLIONAIRE FOR MOLLY
 (Tender Romance™)

BUSHFIRE BRIDE

BY
MARION LENNOX

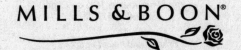

MILLS & BOON®

First published in Great Britain 2004
Harlequin Mills & Boon Limited,
Eton House, 18-24 Paradise Road, Richmond, Surrey TW9 1SR

© Marion Lennox 2004

ISBN 0 263 83913 3

Set in Times Roman 10½ on 12 pt.
03-0804-47978

Printed and bound in Spain
by Litografia Rosés, S.A., Barcelona

PROLOGUE

THE thin blue line rose and fell. Rose and fell. Rose and fell.

How long does love last?

The young woman by the bed should surely know. She sat and watched now as she'd sat and watched for years.

'I love you, Craig,' she whispered, but there was no answer. There was never an answer.

Dappled sunlight fell over lifeless fingers. Beloved eyes, once so full of life and laughter, stayed closed.

The blue line rose and fell. Rose and fell.

'I love you, Craig,' she whispered again, and blessed his face with her fingers. 'My love…'

How long does love last?

For ever?

CHAPTER ONE

'SHE may be beautiful but I bet she's stupid.'

Dr Rachel Harper's hamburger paused midway to her mouth. Tomato sauce oozed onto her T-shirt, but her T-shirt was disgusting already. The sauce was the same colour as her pants. Hey—she was colour co-ordinated!

She was also distracted.

'Look at her hair,' the voice was saying. 'It'd cost a fortune to keep it like that, and what for? She's a blonde bimbo, Toby, mark my words. A gorgeous piece of fluff.'

'But she's got lovely legs.' The child's words were a thoughtful response to the man's deep rumble. 'And she's got really nice eyes.'

'Never be taken in by appearances, Toby,' the deep voice decreed. 'Under that gorgeous exterior, she's nothing but a twit.'

Enough! Rachel might be a reluctant protector, but she was here to defend and defend she would. She hitched back the curtain and faced the world.

Or, to be precise, she faced the Cowral dog show.

The pavilion was packed and she'd retreated with her hamburger for a little privacy. The cubicles behind each dog weren't big enough to swing a cat—or a dog—but at least they were private.

Who was criticising Penelope?

'Hey!' she said, and a man and a child turned to stare. She wiped a smudge of tomato sauce from her chin and stared right back.

Penelope's detractor was in his mid-thirties, she guessed.

Maybe he was a farmer? That's what he looked like. He was wearing moleskins and a khaki shirt of the type that all the farmers around here seemed to wear. His curly black hair just reached his collar. He had deep brown, crinkly eyes and, with his deeply tanned skin, he looked...

Nice, Rachel decided. In fact, if she was being critical—and she was definitely in the mood for being critical—he looked more than nice. He looked gorgeous! The small boy beside him was aged about six, and he was a miniature replica. They had to be father and son.

Father and son. Family. The man was therefore married.

Married? Why was she wondering about married?

She gave herself a swift mental swipe for thinking of any such thing. Dottie had been doing her work too well. Why would Rachel possibly be interested in whether a complete stranger had a partner?

She was here with Michael.

But, then, who was she kidding? She was interested in anyone but Michael—married or not. The fact that she was married herself didn't—couldn't—matter. Dr Rachel Harper had reached her limit.

'I need to show Penelope to gain championship points,' Michael had told her one day at Sydney Central Hospital, where they both worked, and Dottie had pushed her to go. 'Get a life,' she'd said. 'It's time to move on.'

So she'd allowed herself to be persuaded. Rachel had imagined an hour or two displaying a beautiful dog, a comfortable motel in the beautiful seaside town of Cowral and the rest of the weekend lazing at the beach. Maybe Dottie was right. She'd had no holiday for eight years. She was exhausted past imagining. Maybe Dottie's edict that it was time to move on was worth considering.

But Michael's dream weekend had turned out to be just that—a dream. Reality was guilt. It was also a heat wave, a motel that refused to take dogs and an entire weekend guarding Michael's stupid dog from supposedly jealous competitors.

Where was Michael? Who knew? She sighed and addressed Penelope's critics.

'Penelope's been bred from two Australian champions,' she told the stranger and his child, and she glared her very best putting-the-peasants-in-their-places glare.

'She's a very nice dog,' the little boy said. He smiled a shy smile up at Rachel. 'Can I pat her nose?'

She softened. 'Of course you can.'

'She might bite,' the man warned, and Rachel stopped smiling and glared again.

'Stupid dogs bite. Penelope's a lady.'

'Penelope's an Afghan hound.'

'So?'

The man's lips twitched. There was laughter lurking behind those dark eyes and the beginning of a challenge. 'So she's dumb.'

Rachel brightened. A challenge? Great. She'd been here too long. She was bored to screaming point. Anything was better than retreating to her soggy hamburger and yesterday's newspapers.

In truth, what she was aching for was a fight with Michael but he wasn't here. However, this man was the same species—male—and the laughter behind his eyes told her he was fair game.

'You're not only rude,' she told him, her gaze speculative. 'You're also racist.'

He raised his brows and his brown eyes creased into laughing disbelief. 'You're saying she's smart?'

'She's a sweetheart.' Rachel gave the great white hound a hug and then winced as a smear of ketchup soiled the dog's immaculate coat. Whoops. Michael would be out with his pistols.

Where was Michael?

'You don't need to take my word for it,' the man was saying. A small crowd was gathering now. The judging heats were over; final judging wasn't for another two hours and things were slow in the dog shed. Rachel wasn't the only one who was bored. 'There's tests for dog intelligence.'

'You're going to implement the MENSA quiz?'

'Nothing so complicated. Lend me a piece of your hamburger.'

'Lend... Hey, get your own hamburger.'

'It's in the interest of scientific research,' he told her.

'My daddy's a doctor,' the little boy said, as if that explained everything.

'Yeah? Doctor of what?' Rachel grinned down at the kid, beginning to enjoy herself for the first time all weekend. 'It sounds a sneaky way to get some of my hamburger.'

'It's a simple experiment,' the man told her, refusing to be sidetracked. 'See my dog?'

The stalls and their associated sleeping quarters were raised almost three feet above the ground. Rachel peered over the edge. A lean, brown dog of indeterminate parentage gazed back at her. As big as a collie, the mutt was all legs, tail and eyes. As Rachel gazed down at him, he raised his back leg for a weary scratch.

'Charming,' Rachel said. 'Great party trick.'

'Digger doesn't do party tricks.'

She nodded in sympathetic understanding. 'I guess you need to be house-trained to be let into parties.'

The man's grin matched hers. War hadn't just been declared—the first shots had been fired. 'Are you implying Digger's not house-trained?'

'Seeing is believing.' This was OK, she decided. For the

first time since she'd been conned into coming to this last bastion of civilisation, she was having fun. Guilt could be forgotten—for the moment. Penelope against Digger. It was a crazy conversation. She wasn't sure how it had started but she didn't intend to stop. 'Breeding will out,' she declared.

'There's been more gone into Digger's breeding than your mutt's.'

'My mutt's name is Penelope,' she said haughtily. 'And she's no mutt. She comes from long line of Australian champions. Whereas your mutt...'

'Digger also comes from a long line of champions,' the stranger told her. He smiled again, and it was a heart-stopper of a smile. A real killer. 'We're sure there's a piece of champion Border collie in there somewhere, and a champion kelpie...'

'And a champion dachshund?' Rachel watched as Digger's tiny pointy tail stuck straight up. 'Definitely dachshund.'

'That's silly,' the little boy said. 'Dachshunds are long and flat and Digger's high and bouncy.'

'Right.' She was trying not to laugh. Both the man and the boy were entrancing. Two gorgeous smiles. Two sets of deep, dark eyes ready to spring into laughter. She was bored out of her brain and this pair were a diversion sent from heaven.

'So what do we do with my hamburger?' she asked, and the man's smile deepened. Honestly, it was a smile to die for.

'We put it under a feed dish.'

Rachel raised her eyebrows, then shrugged and handed over her burger. A fair amount of ketchup came, too.

The man looked down at his hand—ketchup with hamburger attached. Ugh. In truth it had been a very soggy hamburger and Rachel wasn't all that sorry to lose it. 'You like your burgers well sauced?'

'Yes,' she told him, and went back to glowering.

'My Dad says tomato sauce has too much salt and salt's bad for blood pressure,' the little boy ventured.

'People who say rude things about dogs are bad for blood pressure,' Rachel retorted, and there was a general chuckle from their growing audience. 'So what are you intending to do with my hamburger?'

'Watch.' The man stooped and placed a piece of hamburger underneath an upturned dog dish. Then he stood back and let Digger's lead go slack.

'Dinner,' he said.

Digger looked up at him. Adoring. Then the skinny, brown dog gazed around the crowd as if ensuring each and every eye was on him. He sniffed, placed a paw on top of the dish, crouched down, pushed with the other paw...The dish toppled sideways to reveal the piece of hamburger.

Digger looked around again as if awaiting applause. It came. He received his due and then delicately ate the hamburger.

Uh-oh.

'Now it's Penelope's turn.'

'She'll get dirty,' Rachel said, and there was a trace of worry in her voice. Penelope might be lovely, but her opposition was seriously smart.

'We'll put it up on her platform.' The stranger's smile was growing broader. 'I'll even wipe the ketchup off. Or maybe you could do it on your T-shirt.'

Ouch! 'Watch your mouth.'

Another grin, but the entire pavilion was watching now and he didn't stop. He placed the dish in front of Penelope's nose. He broke a second piece of hamburger, showed it to Penelope and popped it underneath.

He backed away and left her to it.

Penelope sniffed. She sniffed again.

She whined.

She lay down in front of the dish. She stood up and barked. She shoved the dish sideways with her nose and barked again.

Nothing happened. She lay down and whined, pathos personified.

'So your dog's hungrier than mine,' Rachel told him with a touch of desperation, and there was general laughter. 'You must starve Digger.'

'Do I look like a man who'd starve a dog?'

No. He didn't. He looked really nice, Rachel decided, and she wished all of a sudden that she wasn't in soiled jeans and sauce-stained T-shirt, that her mass of deep brown curls were untangled and not full of the straw that the organisers had put down as bedding, and that she looked...

Oh, heck, what was she thinking of? This guy had a kid. She was here with Michael and...

'Rachel, are you feeding Penelope?'

Unthinkingly, she'd raised the feed bowl, and Penelope was launching herself into the hamburger as if there was no tomorrow.

'Um...Michael.'

Michael, silver-haired, suave and in charge of his world, was elbowing through the crowd and his face was incredulous. No one messed with Michael's instructions. Pedigree dog food only. 'What on earth do you think you're doing?'

'I'm proving Penelope's intelligence,' she told him, chin jutting. Enough was enough and she'd had more than enough of Dr Michael Levering.

Back at Sydney Central, Michael had seemed witty and charming and, as one of Sydney's top cardiologists, he was extremely eligible. His invitation to go away with him for the weekend had half the staff in Casualty green with envy, and her friends and her family had finally pushed her to accept. 'Come on,' her mother-in-law had told her. 'This is your chance. You know it's time you moved on. A romantic weekend with a gorgeous bachelor... Rachel, love, you take some precautions and go for it!'

Precautions. Ha! That was the last thing she'd needed. They were supposed to be sharing dog duty. That was another joke. Michael had said he'd sleep in the car because he was too tall to fit in the dog box, but she was starting to have serious doubts about what car he'd slept in. When he'd appeared this morning, ten minutes before Penelope had been due to appear in the judging ring, he'd looked far too clean to have slept in any car. Then he'd said he'd had to make an urgent telephone call. She hadn't seen him again.

So what had he been doing all this time? She looked at him suspiciously, checking for damp hair. If she could prove he'd been swimming while she'd dog-sat, she was going to have to kill him.

'Our dog's more intelligent than yours,' the little boy piped up, and Michael stared down at the child in distaste.

'What are you talking about?'

Rachel flinched. This weekend was definitely not going to plan. Sexy? Eligible? Ha! This man was a king-sized toad.

'I'm Toby McInnes and this is my dad,' the little boy told him, oblivious to the anger in Michael's voice. 'My dad's Dr Hugo McInnes. Who are you?'

Michael opened his mouth but Rachel forestalled him. She knew what would come out and it wouldn't be pleasant. 'This is Michael and I'm Rachel,' she told the little boy. She watched Hugo's grip tighten on his son's hand and she didn't blame him; she was moving into protection mode herself. 'Penelope is Michael's dog.'

But Michael had moved on. He was talking only to Rachel. 'Did you know there are bushfires out of town?'

'Bushfires?' Rachel knew nothing of any bushfires. She hadn't been out of the pavilion all day.

'They're a long way from here.' The man—the doctor?—called Hugo was gazing from Rachel to Michael and back again. His initial anger at Michael seemed to have faded and he now looked as if the whole scene held great interest for him.

'The fires are threatening to block the road,' Michael snapped. He shoved Penelope away from him and the big dog practically fell over. Fast thinking was not Penelope's strong point. She whined a little and nuzzled Rachel, and Rachel gave her a hug. Stupid or not, she was still a very nice dog.

As company went, if Rachel had a choice between Penelope or Michael, Penelope was definitely preferable.

'Rachel, there's an emergency back in town,' Michael was saying. 'Bushfires or not, I need to leave. There's a helicopter on the way to collect me.'

'A helicopter?'

A helicopter. Coming to collect Michael. Rachel focused. She really focused.

Michael was clean-shaven. He was wearing immaculate slacks and a crisp white shirt—and a tie for heaven's sake. And his hair... She couldn't stop staring at his hair. He looked like he'd just emerged from the shower.

The dog pavilion didn't run to showers. Rachel hadn't seen running water for twenty-four hours. She stank of Michael's dog.

What was the bet Michael had just come from the beach via a shower? Via a motel.

She'd reached her limit. His talk of helicopters wasn't making sense but she didn't care.

'Did you sleep at the motel last night?' she demanded, and Michael paused.

'No, but—'

'Do you own a red Aston Martin?' Hugo asked, politely interested.

'Yes.' Michael suddenly looked flustered. Understandably. He was used to deference and subservience. He wasn't finding it here.

'That fits,' Hugo was saying. 'You look the sort of guy who owns an Aston Martin. I did a house call at the motel at two this morning. Arnold Roberts was suffering badly from gout. He had the adjoining suite to yours. We inspected your car from stem to stern while we waited for his analgesic to take effect.' He smiled from Rachel to Michael and back again—as if he was being really, really helpful. 'We were wondering who'd bring a car like that to a place like this and now we know. I'll tell Arnold it belongs to an Afghan owner and all will be clear.'

He was laughing, but Rachel hardly noticed. Her fury was threatening to overwhelm her.

'You slept at the motel?'

Michael heard her anger then. Everybody did.

'I thought you cancelled,' she said carefully. 'When they wouldn't let us bring the dog.'

'They rang me later and said it was too late to cancel—they were keeping my deposit,' Michael muttered. He had the grace to look a bit shamefaced, but only for a moment. He regrouped fast. With an ego the size of Michael's it was easy. 'And by then you'd agreed to sleep here. For heaven's sake, Rachel, you know how small the car is. Do you want me to hurt my back?'

'Yes!'

'Look, it's immaterial anyway,' he told her, moving right

on. 'It's just as well I had a decent night's sleep as it happens. Hubert Witherspoon's had a heart attack.'

Hubert Witherspoon? The name had its desired effect. Rachel's fury was deflected—for the moment.

Hubert Witherspoon was probably the richest man in Australia. He owned half the iron ore deposits in the country. What the man wanted, the man got.

'He wants me,' Michael told her.

'What—?'

'The Witherspoon family aren't risking road blocks due to bushfire. They've sent a helicopter to take me back to Sydney.' He glanced at his watch. 'It should be landing right now and they want me to leave immediately. Can you show Penelope for her final judging and bring her home afterwards?'

Hubert Witherspoon…

Hubert's death would be a national catastrophe—at least for the financial markets. It should have made Rachel's eyes widen in awe.

It should have made her do whatever Michael wanted. But—Michael had been swimming. He'd slept in a motel. In a bed.

While she'd been sitting with Penelope, feeling just dreadful about leaving Sydney. For such a reason…

'You want me to show Penelope?' she managed, and he smiled, the smooth, specialist-to-junior-doctor smile that had persuaded her to come on this weekend in the first place. Why did it make her think suddenly of snake oil?

'You've been watching the other dogs being shown,' he told her. 'You saw how I handled Penelope this morning.' He checked Rachel from head to toe with a judge's critical eye. 'Penelope will be fine. You might want to get yourself cleaned up a bit first, though.'

If she didn't slug him it was only because they were surrounded by a score of onlookers, but it was a really close thing. Somehow she managed to keep hold of a shred of dignity. A scrap. 'Right.' She took a deep breath. 'You want me to drive all the way back to Sydney by myself?'

'Of course. Unless the bushfires block the road. I'll understand if you're delayed.' He tossed her the car keys and she was so astounded she caught them. But that was all she was doing.

'No.'

'Rachel…' His tone became patient-consultant talking to slightly stupid junior. 'You know I can't be replaced. Hubert needs a cardiologist and he needs the best.'

'I have hay in my hair,' she muttered through gritted teeth. 'I can't show a potential Australian champion.'

'Yes, you can. You just need a—'

He got no further. She lifted the car keys and threw them right at his freshly shined shoes. 'Your dog, your problem. I'm going home,' she told him, one syllable at a time. 'I'll hitchhike if I must, but I'm not touching your car.'

'Rachel—'

'Stuff it. Stuff you.'

'But Hubert—'

'Hubert can die for all I care, but he won't die because you're not there. He's over eighty, he's grossly overweight and there are at least five cardiologists in Sydney who are as qualified as you are to care for him.'

'You know that's ridiculous.'

'I know nothing of the kind.'

'Can I make a suggestion?' It was Brown Eyes. Hugo. But Rachel wasn't in the mood for interruptions. She wheeled and gave him a look to kill.

'Butt out. This is my business.'

He held up his hand, placating. 'Whoa…'

'I'm out of here.' She leaned back into the cubicle,

grabbed her overnight bag and hauled it out. It was a fine gesture which didn't come off quite as planned. She hadn't snibbed her bag shut, and it flew open. Out tumbled her spare jeans, her toilet bag—and a bra and a couple of pairs of very lacy, very scant panties.

They were Dottie's offerings. Her mother-in-law. 'You never know what's going to happen, dear,' she'd told her. 'And I do so want you to be prepared.'

Dottie was right. You never did know what was going to happen, but one thing Rachel did know. She'd been a fool to ever agree to come here. She closed her eyes as her belongings tumbled everywhere. A bra flew past Digger's nose. He snagged it and held on, seemingly bemused.

Everyone was bemused.

Dear heaven, let the ground open under her. She had to get out of here.

'The dog can keep it,' she said with as much dignity as she could muster, stuffing the rest of her gear into her bag and fighting a wave of burning mortification. 'He's so smart he can probably work out how to wear it.' She pulled the remains of her bag shut, tugged the shreds of her dignity around her and stalked toward the door.

They watched her go, Hugo with laughter in his eyes and Michael with his jaw somewhere around his ankles.

She didn't care. If she didn't see any one of them again she'd be delighted. She was getting out of here.

She didn't make it.

She stalked out of the pavilion, took a couple of deep breaths and regrouped for a moment to try and figure out the location of the main entrance to the showgrounds—and a dogfight broke out just behind her.

CHAPTER TWO

SHE stopped.

Of course she stopped. The sound of the dogfight was unmistakable, the vicious, ear-splitting snarls breaking through everything else.

And then a high-pitched scream of human terror.

She'd have to have been less than human to ignore it. She turned and stared, as did everyone else close enough to hear.

The dogfight was at the entrance of the pavilion she'd just left and it wasn't a fight—it was a massacre. A faded old cocker spaniel, black and white turned to grey, had been held on its lead by his teenage owner but the pit bull terrier had no restraint and it was intent on killing. The dogs were locked in mortal combat, though the cocker clearly had no idea about fighting—no idea about how to defend himself.

The spaniel's owner—a girl of maybe fifteen or so—was the one who'd screamed in terror. She was no longer screaming. She was trying desperately to separate them. As Rachel started forward—no!—the girl grabbed the pit bull's collar and hauled. The dog snarled and twisted away from the spaniel—and bit.

'No!'

Rachel was screaming at her to stop—to let go. She was running, but it was a good fifty yards back to the entrance to the pavilion.

The man—Hugo—was before her. The dogs were everywhere—a mass of writhing bodies with the girl beneath…

She had to get them apart. The girl would be killed.

19

Rachel dived to grab a collar to pull the pit bull from the girl, but her arm was caught.

'Keep back!' Hugo's harsh command had the power to make her pause. He was reaching for a hose snaking across the entrance and he hauled it forward. 'Turn it on.'

She saw instantly what he wanted and dived for the tap. Two seconds later the tap was turned to full power. The massive hose, used to blast out the mess in the pavilion after showtime, was directed full at the dogs.

Nothing else could have separated them. The blast hit the pit bull square on the muzzle and drove him back. The hose turned to the spaniel, but he was already whimpering in retreat, badly bitten by the pit bull, while Rachel launched herself at the prone body of the girl.

'Her leg…' she breathed.

The girl's leg was spurting bright arterial blood, a vast pulsating stream. Oh, God, had the dog torn the femoral artery? She'd die in minutes.

The dog had lunged at her upper leg and the girl had been wearing shorts! Dear heaven…

'Someone, get my bag. Fast! Run!' Hugo was shouting with urgency. 'The car's by the kiosk.' Car keys were tossed into the crowd—swiftly, because Hugo's hands were already trying to exert pressure. Rachel was hauling her T-shirt over her head. They needed something for a pressure pad—anything—and decency came a very poor second to lifesaving.

She shoved the shirt into Hugo's hands and Hugo wasn't asking questions. He grabbed the T-shirt and pushed.

'Kim, don't move,' Hugo was saying, and with a jolt Rachel realised he was talking to the girl. He was good, this man. Even *in extremis* he found time to tell his patient what was happening. 'Your leg's been badly bitten and we need to stop the bleeding. I know it hurts like hell but someone's gone for painkillers. Just a few short minutes before we can ease the pain for you, Kim. I promise.'

Could she hear? Rachel didn't know and she had to concentrate on her own role. Hugo would want a more solid pad than one T-shirt could provide. She stared up into the crowd. 'Michael,' she yelled. Hugo was too busy applying pressure to haul off his shirt and he needed something to make a pad. And Michael could help with more than a shirt. He had the skills.

But Michael was gone.

It couldn't matter. 'Take mine.' A burly farmer had seen her need and was hauling off his shirt. She accepted with gratitude, coiling it into a pad.

Out of the corner of her eye she saw her overnight bag, sprawled and open in the dust where she'd dropped it as she'd lunged for the tap. More clothes. Great. As Hugo looked up, searching for whatever she had, she handed him a pad. She made another with what was in the bag. Then she shoved the pad hard down over his and pressed. He pressed with her. Even their combined effort wasn't enough to stop the flow.

'I need forceps,' he said grimly. 'My bag…'

'Clive's gone to fetch it,' the farmer told them, hovering over both doctors as they worked, his face ashen with concern. 'He'll be back any minute. He's the fastest runner.'

'Good.' They were working together, their hands in tandem. Hugo was breathing fast, using all his strength to push tighter, and Rachel realised that she was hardly breathing at all. *Live. Please.* It was a prayer she'd learned early on in her medical training, and had used over and over. Skills were good but sometimes more was needed.

Luck?

Still the blood oozed. 'Push down harder,' Hugo told her. 'Don't move off the wound.'

'I'm not moving,' she said through gritted teeth. The bite resembled a shark bite—a huge, gaping wound that, left untended, would release all the body's blood in minutes.

Even if tended…

She was pushing down so hard it hurt.

'I need forceps.' Hugo's voice was growing more urgent as the situation became more desperate. 'Damn, where's my bag?'

'Here.' A youngster, a boy of about sixteen, was bursting through the crowd, carting a bag that was three times the size of any doctor's bag that Rachel had ever seen. A country doctor's bag.

'Haul it open.'

The boy flicked the bag open and Rachel's eyes widened. Forceps. There were several and they were sitting on the top as if prepared for just this emergency. She lifted a hand from the wound and grabbed the first pair.

'We're not going to stop this without clamping,' she muttered. 'The femoral artery has to have been torn to explain this.'

He accepted her medical knowledge without a blink. 'I agree. Clive, take a shirt and clear as much blood as you can while we work. Let's go.' He grabbed forceps himself and then looked across at her. 'Ready?'

She took a deep breath. This was a huge risk. They needed the pad to stop the spurting, but the only way to stop the bleeding altogether was to remove the pad and locate the source. They had only seconds to do it or the girl would die beneath their hands.

'OK.' She took two deep breaths. 'Now.'

They lifted the pad away from the wound. The blood spurted out and they were working blind, searching in the mess that was the girl's leg.

Where in this mess was the artery? Dear God, they had to stop it.

'Take the swab right away, Clive. Just for the moment,' Hugo said. 'Be ready to replace it.'

And in the tiny millisecond before the wound refilled with blood… 'There!' Rachel pushed in and grasped, and the forceps linked to the torn artery. She clicked them shut—and the pumping died.

Not enough.

There were more. As well as the femoral artery, two or three minor vessels had been torn. They could kill all by themselves.

Hugo's forceps clamped shut on another blood vessel and the flow abated still further. Another pair of forceps was in Rachel's hands and Hugo had another.

She was working like lightning. Without the pads there was no pressure—the blood simply pumped out.

'Gotcha.' Another one was under Hugo's forceps. He clamped.

And another.

And that was it.

The blood was still oozing, but slowly now. The pumping had stopped. It'd be flowing from the ripped veins but they'd done what they had to do. For now.

'We need to continue with pressure,' she said, and sat back as Hugo set to work with another shirt, forming another pad. They'd been lucky. Trying to find the blood vessels in these conditions…

Yeah, they'd been lucky—but this man was good!

Hugo was tying the pad firmly around the leg. He gave her a curious glance. There was still urgency but they were working with minutes now rather than seconds. They'd blocked off the blood supply. Now they needed to prevent shock setting in. They needed to replace fluids and they needed to save a leg that no longer had a blood supply.

'Pete, ring the ambulance,' Hugo snapped into the crowd. 'Tell them I want plasma and saline on board and if they're not here in thirty seconds I'll have their hides. Dave, can you and a couple of the men find those damned dogs and deal with them before we have another disaster? Toby… Where's Toby?' He looked out into the crowd, searching for his little boy. 'Myra, can you take him?'

'The first two are already being looked after,' someone said. 'The vet's got the cocker and a couple of guys have gone after the pit bull. The ambulance is on its way.'

Which left Toby.

A middle-aged woman stepped from the crowd of horrified onlookers and took Toby's hand. The child had been standing white-faced and shocked as Hugo and Rachel had worked. 'Come on, love,' she told him. 'Come with me while Daddy looks after Kim.'

Kim…

Rachel looked up to the girl's deathly white face. Kim's eyes were open but it wasn't clear whether she was conscious or not.

'You'll be OK, Kim,' she told her, taking the opportunity to take the girl's hand in hers. What she'd most need now would be reassurance. Not panic. 'We needed to hurt you a bit to stop the bleeding but we're both doctors. We know what we're doing. The bleeding's stopped now.'

The girl's eyes widened. She was conscious.

'Mum… Knickers…'

'Someone find the Sandersons,' Hugo ordered. 'It's OK, Kim. We'll find your mum and dad now, and Knickers is with the vet. You know Rob will look after Knickers just as I'll look after you.'

The flaring panic in the girl's eyes subsided. They were winning. Kind of. For now.

But…was one of the reasons the bleeding had eased because the blood pressure itself had dropped?

'She hasn't lost too much,' Hugo muttered, and Rachel realised he was thinking the same as she was.

Too much blood…

There was certainly a lot. Rachel herself was covered with a spray of gore. She was wearing only a bra above the waist and she looked like something out of a vampire movie. Paramedics were supposed to wear protective clothing, she thought ruefully. If Kim had any sort of blood-borne disease, then she and Hugo were now also infected.

They couldn't care. Not now.

Hugo was swabbing the girl's arm and Rachel moved to get a syringe. By the time Hugo had the line ready she was prepared.

'Five milligrams morphine?'

'Yeah, and then saline. We need plasma. Hell, where's the ambulance?'

It was here. There was a shout and then someone was pushing through the crowd. A couple of ambulance officers.

Rachel almost wept with relief. They'd have plasma, saline—everything Hugo needed.

They'd take over. This wasn't her place. She could go back to being a horrified onlooker.

But…

'Your husband's a cardiologist?' She'd gone back to applying pressure as Hugo inserted an IV line.

Her husband? She stared blankly and then realised who he was talking about. Michael, her husband. What a thought! But now wasn't the time for fixing misconceptions. 'Yes.'

'Thank God for that.'

'Sorry?'

'I'm the only doctor in town,' he told her. 'Can you ask someone to find him? He'll be able to help.'

'He was catching the helicopter back to Sydney,' Rachel said blankly.

'There's a helicopter's taking off now,' a voice said helpfully. 'You can hear it.'

He'd left? Michael had left?

Maybe he hadn't even noticed what had happened. Rachel had stalked out and it'd be just like Michael to have left as well. He'd have heard the dogfight but he wouldn't have turned to investigate. She knew him well enough after this weekend to know he wouldn't deviate from his chosen plan for anyone.

'He's taken the helicopter?' Hugo searched the crowd to find the farmer who'd been the first to offer his shirt. 'OK, it'll have to come back. Matt, get onto the radio. Get the chopper returned here. Tell the pilot we need priority. Kim needs emergency surgery if we're to save this leg. She needs vascular surgeons. We need to evacuate her—now!'

'Will do,' Matt muttered, and ran.

There was a crowd of about twenty onlookers around them now, but it wasn't the sort of crowd you saw in city accidents, Rachel thought. There was horror on everyone's faces. They all knew Kim. They were all desperate to help.

Rachel was the only woman who'd stripped to her bra but she knew without asking that each and every one of these women would do the same and more if they needed to. Their care and concern were palpable.

Then Kim's parents were there, running toward their daughter across the showgrounds. Their fear reached the group on the ground before they did, but Kim had drifted into unconsciousness. The combination of shock, blood loss and painkillers had sent her under. Good, Rachel thought as her mother disintegrated into tears, sobbing onto her chest. The horror on her parents' faces would only have made things worse.

Enough. There was nothing more she could do now. One of the paramedics had taken her position, keeping pressure on the wound. She rose. A buxom woman in floral Crimplene put her arm around her and held. Rachel wasn't complaining. She was grateful for the support.

'Who are you?' Hugo asked. He was adjusting a bag of plasma, the ambulance officers were helping. Rachel wasn't needed.

'Rachel. Rachel Harper.'

'You're a doctor?'

'Yes.'

'You're not a vascular surgeon, I suppose?'

'I wish.' She knew exactly what he was thinking. A vascular surgeon was what they needed, urgently. The chances of saving Kim's leg were incredibly slim. 'But Michael has the skills. And he's still in range.'

He'd be upset at being called back but he had no choice.

'OK.' He stared up at her for a moment longer, his intelligent eyes assessing. Each knew what the other was thinking. They couldn't voice it here—not in front of Kim's parents—but if the femoral artery wasn't repaired fast, Kim would lose the leg if not her life.

They needed the helicopter. They needed Michael. Kim's future depended on it.

There was nothing Rachel could do, though.

For now she was no longer needed.

Mrs Keen, the lady in the Crimplene, ushered Rachel into the showground caretaker's residence. As the ambulance screamed its way to the hospital she was already under hot water while Mrs Keen tut-tutted about the state of her clothes.

'And the clothes in your bag are no better,' she told Rachel through the bathroom door. 'One of the men brought your bag over but you've dropped it, and then used everything to stop the bleeding. Oh, my dear, there's blood on everything.'

That was a minor worry. For now Rachel couldn't care. She let the hot water steam away the gore and she worried about the girl. Worried about the leg.

Michael would be really angry at being recalled. He'd hate to miss out on the Witherspoon case.

It couldn't matter. He wouldn't have heard the dogfight, she decided. Michael Levering saw only the things that affected him. He was needed in Sydney for a prestigious patient and Rachel wasn't doing what he wanted. He'd have simply turned on his heel and stalked away. As for Rachel and Penelope—others could pick up the pieces. If Rachel didn't take his expensive dog and his expensive car back to Sydney, well, Michael had the money to send a lackey to the country to collect them later in the week. Dog-show organisers were hardly likely to let Penelope starve and even if they did…

Penelope was just a possession.

'Damn the man.'

She was shaking, a combination of anger and reaction to the whole situation. They'd been really, really lucky to save Kim's life.

Michael would be back. The helicopter would have returned by now and, dislike Michael as she did, she had to concede he possessed the skills she didn't. He was an incredibly competent vascular surgeon. He might not have noticed the dog fight but if they planned to evacuate Kim on his helicopter, he would, of course, treat her. And with Hugo as back-up...

She washed the last trace of blood from her arms as Mrs Keen's face appeared around the door. Her cheeks were crimson with embarrassment and distress.

'My dear, I'm sorry to disturb you but you're needed back at the hospital. Dr McInnes has just rung. The helicopter's refused to turn around,' she told her. 'Dr McInnes says he has to operate now or she'll lose the leg, and you're all the help he has.'

'It's not a publicly owned chopper.' Harold Keen, the showground caretaker, drove her to the hospital in grim-faced anger. 'It seems it belongs to the chap that had the heart attack—Hubert Witherspoon. His man's the pilot. He's under instructions to take your young man to Sydney and there's no way he's turning back.'

'But Michael's on board. Surely he can overrule.'

'I don't think he has any say in the matter.'

Rachel stared straight ahead. She was wearing one of Doris Keen's Crimplene dresses. She'd hauled a comb through her hair, but her curls were still dripping. She was wearing a pair of Doris's sandals. She was heading to a tiny country hospital where they were facing surgery that was a nightmare.

Help!

'I suppose someone's looking after Penelope,' she said in a small voice, and Harold looked her over with evident approval.

'Your dog's fine,' he told her. 'There's any amount of folk looking after her. You look after Kim and we'll look after you.'

'Thank you.' She felt like she was about to cry. Damn

Michael. Damn him. He had the skills she didn't. He had the helicopter she needed.

He was gone.

'It's no use being angry. We just have to get on with it.'

Hugo was already kitted out for surgery in green theatre gown, cap and slippers. The nurse had ushered Rachel straight through to the theatre. She glanced around and her heart sank. This was a tiny surgery, set up for minor procedures. Not the major trauma that was facing them now.

She swallowed and looked up, and some of her panic must have shown in her face.

'What's your background?' he asked, his voice gentling a little.

'I'm a registrar at Sydney Central. Emergency medicine. I don't... I don't have the surgical skills to cope with this.'

'But you're the reason we were able to clamp the arteries so fast,' he told her. 'So you saved Kim's life in the first place. It's just a matter of finishing what we started.'

Yeah, right. 'You're planning on rejoining the femoral artery?'

'If we can—yes.' He shook his head. 'It may be unlikely we'll succeed but we have to try. I've been on the phone to specialists in Sydney and we don't have a choice. By the time we get her evacuated to Sydney the leg will be dead. If we don't try then she loses the leg. It's as simple as that. I'm assuming you can give an anaesthetic?'

He wasn't expecting her to operate. That was such a relief her knees almost buckled right then.

'Yes.' If he was prepared to be heroic then so was she. This was heroic surgery, she thought. Damn fool surgery. The outcome seemed almost inevitable but he was right. They had to try.

'It's not as bad as it seems,' he told her. 'We have a video link to Sydney. Joe Cartier, one of the country's leading vascular surgeons, has agreed to help us every step of the way. I've hauled in Jane Cross, a local who plays at being a film-maker. She's setting up computer equipment and she'll video while we operate. She can do really intricate close-up stuff so everything I do goes straight down the line to Sydney and I get immediate feedback.'

He'd organised all this while she'd been in the shower?

'I... You're not a surgeon?'

'I'm a family doctor,' he told her. 'I'm two hours away from back-up. I'm everything. If you weren't here—if I didn't have an anaesthetist—then I'd count this impossible. But we have enough going for us now to hope. So what are we waiting for? Let's go.'

Afterwards, when Rachel was asked to describe what had been done, she'd simply shake her head. How they did it...It was impossible. All she could describe were the technicalities, and they were impressive enough.

They had a speaker-phone mounted just beside the table. Every sound they made went straight down the wire to Sydney.

Jane Cross, a woman in her forties, looking crazily incongruous with theatre garb covering a purple caftan and a mass of jangling earrings dangling beneath her theatre cap, directed a video camera straight at the wound.

'You promise you won't faint?' Hugo had asked the middle-aged woman as she'd set up the equipment, and Jane had regarded Hugo and Rachel with incredulity. Even with a hint of laughter.

'What, faint? Me? When I've got a captive audience? I intend to faint at least three times and I'll probably throw up too, but later. Not until I've done my job.'

She was wonderful, Rachel decided. She was right there

behind Hugo's hands, but somehow she had the skill and the sensitivity to stay clear enough for his fingers to do their work.

The pictures she took were via a digital video camera linked to video conferencing equipment. In Sydney Joe Cartier had a clear view—and Hugo was asking questions every step of the way.

Rachel couldn't help him at all. She had her own battles. She wasn't a trained anaesthetist—she'd done basic training but that was all—and Kim was so severely shocked that just keeping her alive was a major battle.

She worked with a phone link, too. They'd run out of phone lines but Jane's partner, a dumpy little woman in jeans and sweatshirt, sat in a corner of the theatre where she didn't have to see—her stomach was evidently not as strong as Jane's—and relayed Rachel's questions down the line to an anaesthetist in Sydney.

'Minimal anaesthesia for such a shocked patient,' the specialist told her, working her through a careful, haemodynamically neutral induction method. He worked through her needs with her and Rachel wondered that such a small hospital could meet the requirements he snapped down the phone.

It could. For a tiny hospital Hugo had brilliant equipment. It was stunning that they had sufficient blood supplies on hand, but there was so much more. Rachel had blood on request, she had plasma, she had saline and a team outside the theatre was warming all the fluids before she even saw them.

The fluids weren't the only thing being heated.

'Keep the patient warm at all costs,' the anaesthetist barked down the phone, and warmed blankets appeared like magic to cover every part of Kim's body that Hugo didn't need to work on. After that one instruction Rachel didn't need to worry about warming—the blankets were replaced every few minutes by freshly warmed ones handed through the door. There must be a hive of industry out there.

It was an amazing scene. As well as the unseen industry outside, they had two nurses working with them in the theatre.

Elly was a competent middle-aged woman, white-faced and shocked because she was best friends with Kim's mum, but that fact wasn't allowed to get in the way of her professionalism. Then there was David, a ginger-headed kid who looked like he was hardly old enough to be qualified—but was magnificent under pressure.

They were all magnificent under pressure, Rachel thought. The whole town.

And Hugo…

What was being asked of him was unthinkable. His concentration was fierce—he didn't lift his head. He concentrated as she guessed he'd never concentrated in his life.

Where was the laughing man at the dog show? Gone. He'd been replaced by a pure professional—a professional being asked to work well past his level of training.

This was nightmare stuff. The specialist at the end of the phone could only guide—there was no way anyone could help Hugo manoeuvre the fine particles of tissue back into being a viable blood supply.

Rachel, concentrating fiercely on an anaesthetic that was taking her to the limits of her ability, could only wonder. If Hugo hadn't been there, could she have done such a thing?

No, she thought honestly. Hugo had obviously done far more extensive reading and studying in this area than she had. The questions he asked the specialist showed keen intelligence and an incisive knowledge of what he was trying to achieve.

The man was seriously good.

And he was succeeding.

Even when the femoral artery was somehow—amazingly—reconnected and the first surge of pink started to appear in the lower leg, he didn't relax. His questions to the unknown Joe in Sydney seemed, if anything, to increase. He worked on and on, tying off vessels that were damaged beyond repair.

He completed the vascular surgery, took a deep breath, and a plastic surgeon came on the line, guiding him through the complex steps in closing such a wound to give a decent cosmetic outcome.

They were worrying about appearances, Rachel thought jubilantly, watching the colour seep back into Kim's toes and making sure the heart line on her monitor stayed steady as blood pressure stabilised. They were worrying how she'd look in the future.

They were winning!

And finally—finally, after hours without lifting their heads—the team in Sydney let out a cheer down the phone lines.

'Well done, Cowral,' they told them. 'Unless you have any more big dogs menacing the populace, we'll leave you to it.'

And to the thanks of the entire theatre team, the telephone lines went dead.

The theatre fell silent. Rachel was still concentrating. Hugo was placing dressings around the wound and she had to concentrate on reversing the anaesthetic, having Kim re-establish her own breathing. But the satisfaction…

She glanced up and the joy she felt was reflected in every face in the room.

Except Hugo's. He looked sick. The strain Rachel had been under had been immense—the strain Hugo had felt must have been well nigh unbearable. He'd won, but at a cost.

She'd worked as a team member for long enough to know that it was time for someone else to take charge. And she was the only possible option.

'David, take over the dressing,' she ordered. 'Hugo, leave the rest to us. We don't need you here any more.' He'd been under more pressure than any doctor should face and now, job done, reaction was setting in with a vengeance.

'I'm OK.' But the hands holding the pad were suddenly shaking. His fingers had seemed nerveless for hours, skilled and precise past understanding. It was more than understandable that reaction should set in now.

'Go and tell the Sandersons their kid will keep her leg,' she told him. 'Kim's parents will still be worried sick. Go.' Kim was taking her first ragged breaths. One of the nurses had given them the news some time ago that their daughter would be fine, but they wouldn't believe it until they'd heard it from Hugo.

And Hugo needed to tell them. Hugo had achieved the impossible. This was his gift.

The theatre team agreed. David lifted the tape from Hugo's nerveless fingers and started applying it. Job done.

'You're being kicked out of Theatre, Dr McInnes,' the young nurse told him, giving his senior a cheeky grin that was still flushed with triumph. They were all high on success. It was a fabulous feeling. 'The lady's told you to leave and what the lady wants the lady should get. Don't you agree?'

Hugo stepped back from the table. He gave Rachel a long, assessing look and then his face broke into the beginnings of a crooked smile.

'I guess. We owe the lady big time.'

'There you go, then,' Rachel said with a lot more placidity than she was feeling. 'Pay your debt to us all by getting out of here.'

'If you're sure.'

'I'm sure.' And then for some reason she couldn't fathom she put her hand on his arm. It was a fleeting gesture—of congratulation?—of comfort? She wasn't sure but she knew that she was compelled to do it.

Her hand stayed. He looked down at her fingers resting on the sleeve of his theatre gown and his face twisted into an expression she didn't recognise. For one fleeting moment his hand came up to cover hers. Warmth flooded between them—and something else. Something she couldn't begin to recognise.

'You're right, Dr Harper,' he said softly, so softly she could hardly catch the words. 'I need to get out of here.'

He left. The two nurses wheeled Kim through to Recovery and Rachel was left with Jane, the lady with the video, and Pat, the lady on the floor holding the mobile phone.

They'd never met until three hours ago and they were grinning at each other like fools.

'That was fantastic,' Rachel said, and if she couldn't keep her voice steady, who could blame her? 'Jane, I have no idea how you filmed that without fainting.'

'Fainting isn't what I felt like,' Jane admitted. 'What I felt like was far more messy. But I figured I could do the messy stuff afterwards when no one needed me and, hey, guess what? Now I don't feel like it at all any more.'

'You realise you guys saved Kim's leg.' The video recording and computer link had meant the specialists on the end of the line had been able to watch them every step of the way and Pat's relayed instructions had given Rachel every skill she'd needed.

'We all saved Kim's leg,' Pat decreed. She rose and came

across to give her friend a hug and then the two of them hugged Rachel. This wasn't something that'd happen in a big city hospital but it was an entirely appropriate action here. A great action. 'We make a fantastic team,' Pat said roundly. 'We're so glad you're here now, Dr Harper. Something tells me Dr McInnes is going to need the best team he can get.'

The words somehow broke through her exhaustion. They didn't make sense. What was Pat saying? Something about Hugo needing a team? Surely that need was past.

'Why now?' she asked. 'Why would Hugo need me any more now?'

'A really solid medical team is exactly what we're going to need now,' Pat told her. 'The wind's swung around. Word came through as we were on our way in here. The fire's blocking the highway. There's no way in and there's no way out, and the fire's getting bigger by the minute.'

Rachel walked through to the sink and hauled off her theatre gown without even thinking. She was so tired she could hardly stand. She ran cold water over her wrists and then splashed her face, trying to haul her tired mind into gear.

She was stuck in this town?

'Well done, you.' The voice behind her made her jump and she turned to find Hugo in the doorway. The exhaustion in his face matched hers.

'Well done, yourself,' she managed. He'd startled her. More… He unnerved her.

He really did have a gorgeous smile, she decided. Crooked but nice. And the way he'd touched her…

No. She didn't want to think about the way he'd touched her.

What was a doctor like Hugo—a doctor with such skills—doing in a place like this? The surgery he'd just performed had been amazing. He should have trained in surgery. He could be one of the country's finest.

'I like Cowral,' he told her, and her eyes widened.

'What…?'

'You were thinking what's a nice boy like me doing in a place like this?' he told her, and he was so near the truth that she gasped.

'I don't… I wasn't…'

'It's what all city doctors think. Why on earth would anyone practise in such a remote area? But I think that Cowral's fantastic. I'm here through choice. While you, Dr Harper, are truly stuck.'

At some time since she'd kicked him out of the operating suite he'd hauled off his theatre gown. Underneath he was wearing moleskins and a casual shirt similar to the ones he'd been wearing at the dog show, though without the gore. Somehow he'd found time to change before surgery. He was transformed again, she thought. Doctor to farmer.

Doctor to farmer? What was she thinking? she wondered. She was finding it hard to concentrate on what mattered.

The fires. Being stuck here.

Craig…

Oh, God, she shouldn't be here.

She was here. She was trapped. Without Craig.

'The fires are bad?'

'The fires are a problem,' he told her. He was splashing cold water on his face as if he needed to wake himself up, and his voice was muted. 'The burn's in the national park. There's no private property threatened but the neck of land into town has been cut. When the fire shifted, everyone who wasn't local got out of town before the road closed. You were in Theatre when the evacuation call came through. We didn't give you that option.' He rubbed his face on a towel and then looked at her. Really looked at her. And his voice softened. 'I'm sorry, Rachel, but you're stuck here for the duration.'

She swallowed and tried to think through the implications. 'We could get helicopter evacuation,' she said at last, and he nodded. Still watching her.

'We could. If it was urgent. But Kim's no longer an urgent case. Are you urgently required back in Sydney?'

Was she urgently needed?

No, she had to admit. At least, not by the hospital. As of last Friday she was officially on holiday. The trip to Cowral had been intended to be a weekend away followed by two weeks of lying in the sun. Back in Sydney, though. She'd have lain on Bondi beach so she could still visit Craig morning and night.

Craig needed her.

No. Craig didn't need her. She needed to get her head around that, once and for all.

She couldn't. But the reality was that no one would complain if she wasn't back in Sydney for the next few days, least of all Craig. She may as well admit it.

'Um…no.'

'That's great,' he told her. 'Because I may just need you myself.'

Hugo needed her. Great.

Everyone needed Rachel. Everyone always had. So what was new?

Dear God, she wanted to go home. Craig…

She didn't have a choice. She was here. With Hugo. While Craig was…

Craig just was.

CHAPTER THREE

RACHEL walked slowly back to the showgrounds, dragging her feet in too-big sandals. She'd told Hugo she needed to see to Penelope. Kim's parents were needing more reassurance. He'd been distracted and she'd slipped away.

He had enough to worry about without her worries. Which were considerable.

It was just on dusk. The evening was still and very, very warm. The sound of the sea was everywhere.

Cowral was built on a bluff overlooking the Southern Ocean. The stars were a hazy sheen of silver under a smoky filter. To the north she could see the soft orange glow of threatening fire. It was too far away to worry about, she thought. Maybe it'd stay in the national park and behave.

Meanwhile, it'd be a great time for a swim. But she had things to sort. Penelope. Accommodation.

Sleep!

Michael's Aston Martin was parked at the entrance to the showgrounds and she looked at it with a frown. She'd thrown the car keys back at Michael. Were they in his pocket right now as he did his heroic lifesaving thing back in the city, or had he left the keys in Penelope's dog stall?

It was all very well standing on one's dignity, she thought ruefully, but if he'd taken his keys then she'd be walking everywhere. She didn't like her chances of hot-wiring an Aston Martin.

Meanwhile… Meanwhile, Penelope. Rachel pushed open the wire gates of the dog pavilion and went to find the second of her worries.

Michael might have taken his car keys but he hadn't taken his dog. Penelope was right where Rachel had left her, sitting in the now empty dog pavilion, gazing out with the air of a dog who'd been deserted by the world.

'Oh, you poor baby.' She hugged the big dog and hauled herself up into the stall to think about her options. 'I haven't deserted you, even if your master has.'

Penelope licked her face, then nosed her Crimplene in evident confusion.

'You don't like my fashion sense either?' She gave a half-hearted smile. 'We're stuck with it. But meanwhile…'

Meanwhile, she was hungry. No. Make that starving! She'd had one bite of a very soggy hamburger some hours ago. The remains had long gone.

Penelope didn't look hungry at all.

'You ate the rest of my hamburger?

Penelope licked her again.

'Fine. It was disgusting anyway, but what am I supposed to eat?' She gazed about her. The pavilion was deserted.

Michael hadn't left his keys.

Her bag was over at the caretaker's residence where she'd showered. She could walk over there and fetch it, but why? The contents of the bag were foul. She had her purse with her—she'd tucked it into a pocket of the capacious Crimplene. She needed nothing else.

Wrong. She needed lots of things.

She had nothing else.

So… She had her purse, a dog and a really rumbling stomach.

'I guess we walk into town,' she told Penelope. The only problem was that the hospital and the showgrounds were on one side of the river and the tiny township of Cowral was on the other.

'We don't have a choice,' she told the dog. 'Walking is

good for us. Let's get used to it. The key to our wheels has just taken himself back to Sydney and we're glad he has. Compared to your master... I hate to tell you, Penelope, but walking looks good in comparison.'

Cowral was closed.

It was a tiny seaside town. It was Sunday night. All the tourists had left when the roads had started to be threatened. Rachel trudged over the bridge and into town to find the place was shut down as if it was dead winter and midnight. Not a shop was open. By the time she reached the main street the pall of smoke was completely covering the moon and only a couple of streetlights were casting an eerie, foggy glow through the haze.

'It looks like something out of Sherlock Holmes,' Rachel told her canine companion. 'Murderer appears stage left...' She stood in the middle of the deserted street and listened to her stomach rumble and thought not very nice thoughts about a whole range of people. A whole range of circumstances.

Murder was definitely an option.

Her phone was in her purse. She hauled it out and looked at it. Who could she ring?

No one. She didn't know anyone.

She stared at it some more and, as if she'd willed it, it rang all by itself. She was so relieved she answered before it had finished the first ring.

'Rachel?' It was Dottie's bright chirpiness sounding down the line. Her mother-in-law who'd so wanted this weekend to work. 'Rachel, I hope I'm not intruding but I so wanted to know how it was going. Where are you, dear?'

Rachel thought about it. 'I'm standing in the main street of Cowral,' she said. 'Thinking about dinner.'

'Oh…' She could hear Dottie's beam down the line. 'Are you going somewhere romantic?'

'Maybe outdoors,' Rachel said, cautiously looking around at her options. 'Under the stars.' She looked through the smoke toward the sea. 'On the beach?'

'How wonderful. Is the weather gorgeous?'

Rachel tried not to cough from smoke inhalation. 'Gorgeous!'

'And you have such gorgeous company.'

Rachel looked dubiously down at Penelope. 'Yes. Yes, I do.'

'You know we so wanted you to have a good time, Lewis and I. There's no chance of extending your time there, I suppose?'

'Actually, there may be,' Rachel told her. She explained about the fires and the road being cut. 'There's nothing to worry about but…we may be held up here for a few more days.' There was no reason to explain that 'we' meant Rachel and an Afghan hound. Not Rachel and a gorgeous hunk of eligible cardiologist.

But her words were just what Dottie wanted to hear. 'Oh, my dear, that's lovely.' She could hear Dottie's beam widen. 'Unless the fires are a real problem?'

'They don't seem to be.' Australians understood about bushfires. Most national parks burned every few years or so—they needed to burn to regenerate—and as long as they didn't threaten townships they weren't a worry. Dottie clearly thought this time they'd been sent from heaven.

'Dottie,' she said cautiously. 'Craig…'

'You're not to worry. We told you and we meant it. His father and I have taken right over as we should have long ago. As you should have let us.'

'But—'

'You concentrate on yourself,' Dorothy told her. 'You

concentrate on your future. On your romantic dinner under the stars. That's an order.'

And the phone went dead.

Great.

She stared at it. Her link with home.

She should be back in the hospital right now. Why wasn't she? Craig…

Don't think about it. Think about now.

Now what?

If there was no dinner to be had in Cowral then she needed to think about her next need. Sleep. Accommodation.

Cowral Bay's only motel—the place where Michael-the-rat had slept last night—was on the other side of the river.

She'd walk back over the bridge, she decided. She'd leave Penelope in her dog box in the pavilion and book herself into the motel. Hey, maybe the motel even had room service.

By the time she reached the motel her feet, in her borrowed sandals, were screaming that she had blisters. She'd bother with taking Penelope back to the pavilion later, she decided, so she tied the dog to a tree and walked into Motel Reception. To find no room at the inn.

'Sorry, love,' the motel owner told her, casting a nervous glance at Rachel's dubious apparel. 'There's fire crews from the other side of the peninsula trapped here now and they've booked us out.'

'Do you have a restaurant?' Rachel asked with more hope than optimism, and was rewarded by another dubious look and another shake of the head.

'Everyone's closed. The Country Women's Association are putting on food twenty-four hours a day for the firefighters in the hall over the bridge but you don't look like a firefighter.'

Rachel swallowed. 'No. No, I don't.'

'Are you OK, love?' the woman asked. Her eyes narrowed. 'You don't need one of them women's refuge places, do you? I could call the police for you if you like.'

Great. That was all she needed. A girl had some pride but Rachel was really struggling to find it here. She took a deep breath and pulled herself together.

Maybe women's refuges had food?

Good grief. What was she thinking?

'Um, no. Thank you.' She fished in her purse and found a couple of coins. There was a candy dispensing machine by the counter and the sweets looked really inviting. 'I'll ring a friend, but meanwhile I'll just buy a couple of these…'

'I'm sorry, love,' the woman told her. 'The machine's broken. The technician's due tomorrow—if he can get through the fires.'

Rachel walked outside and untied Penelope. Then she considered, trying really hard not to panic.

Panic seemed an increasingly enticing option.

She'd go back to the hospital, she decided. Hugo had said he needed her. How much? He was about to be put to the test. 'If you need me you'll have to house and feed me,' she'd tell him.

'No. Feed me first,' she corrected herself.

And Penelope?

Maybe she couldn't expect Hugo to take on Penelope. She'd take her back to the pavilion.

Bad idea. It had been almost an hour now since Rachel had collected Penelope. Penelope had been the last dog to leave and the showground caretakers had done their duty. At some time while Rachel had walked into town and back again, the high wire gates had been bolted closed.

The caretaker's residence was in the centre of the grounds, well out of shouting distance.

Rachel put her head against the cyclone wire and closed her eyes. Great. Just great. The whole situation was getting farcical.

Where was this women's refuge?

'This has to go into the record books as the most romantic weekend a girl has ever had,' she told Penelope, but Penelope looked at her with the sad eyes of an Afghan hound who hadn't been fed.

'You ate my hamburger,' Rachel told her. 'Don't even think about looking at me like that.'

She sighed. Her stomach rumbled a response. She put her hand on Penelope's collar and started trudging toward the hospital.

There was the sound of vehicle behind her—a big one. She moved onto the verge.

A fire truck came around the bend on the wrong side of the road. It veered onto the grassy verge and she had to jump for her life.

If she'd been one whit less angry she might have been hit, but her reflexes were working fine. Rachel was tired and hungry and worried, but there was still a vast well of anger directed at Michael and herself and her circumstances. When the fire truck swerved around the bend on the wrong side of the road it was almost as if she expected it.

She yelped and leapt, and as the truck screeched to a halt she found herself sprawled ignominiously in the grass at the side of the road with Penelope somehow sprawling on top of her.

Great. What else could possibly happen to her? She lay

and addressed herself to a clump of grass right under her nose.

'Beam me up, Scottie. Where's a spaceship when you need one?'

'Are you OK, miss?' The horror in the voice above her had her pushing herself up from the road. She might be mad as fire but no one here deserved to think they'd squashed her.

'I'm fine.' She rolled over, shoved a startled Penelope off, hauled her Crimplene down to something akin to decency and tried to look fine. 'Honest.'

'Oh, heck...' The man had reached her. He'd been driving the truck. Behind him his fellow firefighters were climbing down from the cab to see what was wrong. The engine was still running and the truck lights were illuminating the road. 'I could have killed you.'

'It's your lucky day. You didn't.' She tried a smile and the muscles almost worked. Sort of.

They were gathering round her now, a bunch of men and women with black-grimed faces, fire uniforms and hard hats. They looked exhausted. They were looking at her with concern.

She must look a real candidate for her women's refuge, she thought, and the concept was looking more and more appealing. If there was a women's refuge somewhere around here that would take her with an Afghan hound, she'd be in there like a shot.

Or maybe... She gave Penelope's backside another shove... Maybe even without an Afghan.

'We're really sorry,' the fireman told her, and she tried focusing on the man before her. He looked scared to death.

'I guess you weren't expecting hikers,' she told him. 'It's too dark to walk off the road.' She hauled herself upward. Someone gave her a hand which she accepted with gratitude. Then she looked more closely at the man before her. Under the soot there were cuts and scratches, blood as well as grime. He looked dreadful. 'Are you OK?'

Stupid question, really. It was absolutely obvious that he wasn't. 'I just…' He wiped his hand across his eyes. 'My eyes… The smoke…'

And he'd been driving.

'You need to go to the hospital,' she told him.

'That's where we're going. There was a shed—the farmer told us it was used for storing hay so we made an attempt to save it. What he forgot to tell us was that he stored fuel in there as well. The thing went up with a bang that scared us almost as much as we scared you. But that's all the damage, thank God. There's a few of us with sore eyes, but we're thinking that we've been lucky.'

Lucky or not, they looked shocked and ill. Rachel's personal problems were set aside in the face of these peoples' needs. 'You should have been treated before you drove.'

'Doc's been busy,' someone said. 'We heard up on the ridge that he couldn't come up. He's been caught up with a dogbite or something.'

Of course he'd been caught up. And there was no one else, Rachel thought. He was on his own.

Except for her. Hugo had her, whether he liked it or not. And a fat lot of use she was, she thought ruefully, hiking round the country with her crazy Afghan hound, looking for food and for shelter as if she were destitute. It was time she hauled herself together and started being useful.

'Tell you what,' she said, brushing gravel from her knees and trying to stop her knees from doing the shaking they were so intent on. 'Let's all go to the hospital. I'm a doctor and I'm needed there. But if it's OK with you…' She managed a shaky grin as she looked around their smoke-filled eyes which were now tinged with disbelief. A doctor in

Crimplene... But she wasn't going down that road. Explanations could take hours.

'Indulge me with something I've always wanted to do,' she told them. 'I'm a country girl from way back. Once upon a time I even drove my dad's truck at hay-carting so I have my heavy vehicle licence. So all you have to do is say yes. Let me drive your fire engine.'

Which was how Dr Rachel Harper, MD, dressed in glorious Crimplene and Doris Keen's sandals, with gravel in her knees, nothing in her stomach and dog hair all over her, got to drive the Cowral Bay fire truck with a bunch of ten disgustingly dirty and slightly injured firefighters and one potential Australian champion Afghan in the back.

You told me to have a weekend to remember, she silently told her absent mother-in-law as they headed for the hospital. Well, Dottie, I'm doing just that.

Hugo wasn't at the hospital, and Rachel was aware of a stab of disappointment. But at least the nurses knew her from that afternoon when she'd helped with Kim. They greeted her as a friend, and the orderly took over Penelope's care as if she was no trouble at all.

'You've come to help, miss,' he told her as the firefighters milled around the emergency room, and it was obvious to everyone that Rachel needed to turn into a doctor again. 'You're very welcome. I'll give your dog some dinner, shall I?'

Dinner... Yes!

'Actually, I—'

But dinner wasn't her destiny. 'It's great that you're here.' David, the ginger-haired nurse who'd helped with Kim, was looking more flustered than he had that afternoon. 'One of our old farmers had a stroke an hour ago. Dr

McInnes had to go out there in a hurry and here's all these guys needing checking. Can I give you a hand and we'll see what we can do together?'

She worked for an hour. It was solid medicine but straightforward, washing out eyes, checking bruises and cleaning scratches. One of the women was suffering slightly from smoke inhalation and Rachel decreed that she be admitted, but the oxygen alleviated the symptoms almost immediately. Great. She worked steadily through on. Minor stuff.

Except the man who'd been driving the truck. He had a sliver of something nasty in his eye as well as a cut that was deep enough to need stitching. But it was the eye she was worried about.

Rachel shoved her rumbling stomach aside and focused.

She dropped in fluorescein—a yellow stain—and examined the eye through the ophthalmoscope. And worried.

'Can we X-ray?' she asked David.

'Sure.'

The X-ray came back—still worrying. She pinned it against the light and fretted some more as the door opened behind her.

'Problem?'

She turned and it was Hugo. For a moment—for just a moment—it was as much as she could do not to fall into his arms with relief. She'd pushed hunger and exhaustion and shock away but the events of the day were catching up with her. She was really close to breaking point.

Falling into a colleague's arms wasn't exactly professional. She got a grip. Sort of. Mental slap around the ears. She hauled herself into as much of a medical mode as she could muster.

'There's a foreign body just at the edge of the cornea,' she told him, turning back to the light-box and attempting to concentrate on the image. 'There was fuel in metal drums that exploded while they were trying to save a shed. This looks like a sliver of metal, embedded in the cornea but not penetrating. His sight's blurred but maybe that's just the reaction to the pain and a bit of debris that's on the surface. The eye won't stop watering. There's a couple of nasty lacerations around the eye itself that'll need stitching but it's the metal I'm worried about. It's very near the optic nerve. If he moves while I'm trying to manoeuvre it out… Well, I don't think I can cope with this under local anaesthetic.'

Hugo nodded. He crossed to stand beside her and they stared at the screen together.

'It's not touching anything crucial. I think we could do it.' He stared at it a bit longer. 'Maybe you're right, though. It's going to be fiddly.'

'But under a local anaesthetic?'

'I'd rather not.' He looked down at her and smiled. 'Like you, ophthalmology isn't my speciality. It looks straightforward enough as long as he doesn't move, but there's a bit of repair work to do and I'm not super-confident. Eyes aren't my area of expertise and if I have to fiddle and curse I'd prefer that the patient was sedated while I did it.'

'That makes two of us.' She looked at the X-ray some more and even managed a shaky smile. 'We couldn't evacuate him to the city?'

'It's a very small sliver. It's not penetrating. Evacuating means bringing a helicopter from the city and visibility is making things dangerous.'

'Yes, but—'

'But we do have two doctors,' he went on inexorably. 'Even if one of them looks like she just came out of a welfare shop.'

'From a home for battered women actually,' she said with

dignity. 'I've had one offer to take me there in a squad car already tonight.'

'Have you?' The ready laughter she was starting to know flashed into his eyes. 'The fire guys tell me they nearly ran you down.'

'Yeah, but then they let me drive their fire engine,' she told him. 'Which was really cool.'

The deep smile lurking in the back of his eyes strengthened into the beginnings of something that looked like pure admiration. And surprise. She flushed but his eyes were sliding down to her legs, breaking the moment. He'd seen her bloodstained knee. 'That graze wants washing.'

'And we all need dinner and a sleep and it's not going to happen,' she told him, still strangely flushed. What was it with this man that had the capacity to unsettle her? She had to move on. 'Our firefighter has an empty stomach which means he's ready for anaesthesia now,' she told him. 'His eye isn't going to get better on its own. If we're going to operate there isn't a better time than now. Is there?'

'Nope.' He sighed. 'I guess not. Lead on, Dr Harper. Do you want to operate or do you want to do the anaesthetic?'

'I'm choosing anaesthetics,' she told him. 'Two anaesthetics in one day! I think I'm starting to specialise.'

It took longer than they had thought it would.

By the time they finished and the firefighter was recovering in the ward, neatly stitched, foreign body removed and intravenous antibiotics preventing complications, Rachel was swaying on her feet. She hadn't felt it at all while she'd been in Theatre—adrenaline again, she supposed—but when she emerged she sagged. Her stocks of adrenaline must be at an all-time low. She crossed to the sinks and held on, and if she hadn't held on she would have sunk to the floor.

It'd pass. She'd worked exhausted in the past. After nights on duty when Craig—

No. Don't go there.

In a minute she'd start considering the complications surrounding her but for now...

For now she held on.

'Hey.' Hugo had hauled off his gown and was watching her, his eyes narrowing in concern. 'Are you OK?'

She thought about it. OK? People kept asking her that and the concept was ludicrous. 'If you're offering to take me back to my women's refuge, the answer is yes.'

'Women's refuge...'

'Any sort of refuge,' she muttered. 'As long as it serves dinner. Bread and dripping would be fine. Come to think about it, bread and dripping would be fantastic.'

'You're hungry.'

'You stole my hamburger—remember?'

'So I did.' He was looking at her as if she'd just landed from outer space. 'That was—what—eight hours ago?'

'It feels more. And I didn't eat it then. Penelope finished it for me. Someone took her off to feed her when I arrived. I bet she's had a really good meal. Doggos or something. Something really delicious.'

'What did you do between operating on Kim and now?' he asked and she rolled her eyes.

'I walked. I walked in these really stupid sandals which, by the way, are about ten sizes too big. I walked back to the pavilion to find Michael hadn't left me the keys to his car. I brought his stupid dog from the pavilion and I walked into town searching for a café to discover the whole place has shut. It's like a ghost town. I walked back to the motel to discover the place has been booked out by the Boys' Own Fire Brigade and their restaurant doesn't serve meals. And their candy-vending machine is broken. I walked back to the showgrounds to discover the gates had been locked. I started to walk back here but the fire engine nearly ran me down. I came in here, I washed out a few eyes, I sewed up a gashed leg and now I've operated on an eye. So... I think maybe I've reached my limit. I'm wearing Doris Keen's Crimplene, my feet hurt, my stomach's empty, I don't even have a dog box to sleep in and I'm very, very close to hysterics.' She eyed him with caution. 'And if you dare to even twitch the sides of your mouth with the suggestion of laughter, Dr McInnes, I intend to lie down on the floor and give way to a full-scale tantrum. They'll hear me back in Sydney.'

'I'm not...' His mouth definitely twitched but it was hauled back under control fast. 'I'm not laughing.'

'I don't believe you.'

'I'm definitely not.' He bit his lip, pushed the laughter resolutely to the backburner and eyed her with a certain amount of caution. 'OK. It appears you need some help. Where shall we start?'

'Food,' she told him.

'As bad as that?'

'Worse.'

'Let's go, then.' He smiled. 'It fits with what I need to do,' he told her. 'I'm hungry, too.'

'You haven't had dinner?'

'One of my very elderly patients had a stroke. I've been out there with her. She died an hour ago.'

'I'm sorry.'

'Don't be,' he told her. 'Annie was a ninety-six-year-old farmer. She's run her own farm since her husband walked out on her sixty years ago. She didn't miss him a bit. She's had a great life; she was healthy and happily living in her own home until the end, and I wish all endings could be as happy.'

'Mmm.'

It was a happy ending. But his words had caught her unawares, twisting her thoughts back to where her thoughts always ended.

Craig…

She swallowed. She looked down at her hands and found her hands had clenched into fists. Craig…

For some stupid reason her eyes were filling with tears.

Which was ridiculous. Surely she should be used to this by now. It was just that she'd never been away. For eight years…

Food. She needed food. That's why she was reacting like this. Hugo was watching her with concern and she blinked and sniffed and got on with it.

'Sorry,' she told him. 'I was just…reacting to the day or something. Did you say you knew where we can find some food?'

He was still watching her, still with that look that said he saw far more than she wanted him to, but he accepted that she needed to move on.

'We'll give you a few biscuits and cheese to keep the wolf from the door while I wash your knee first,' he told her. 'I need a medico with two good legs—not with one infected. Then we find Toby. Toby's down at the town hall, and that's where the food is. There's a fire effort happening in town and the locals are either out on the front or working to support them. Even at this late hour there'll be food. So we'll collect Toby and feed you. Two birds with one stone.'

She blinked back the last of her emotion and managed a grin.

'Lead on, then,' she told him. 'Two birds, did you say? I'll eat them both.'

That he'd noticed the embedded gravel in her knee amazed her. The Crimplene was flapping around her calves and her knees were hardly exposed. Maybe one of the firefighters had told him.

Or maybe he'd just…noticed? He was that sort of a doctor, she decided as he carefully scrubbed the surface and then checked that each particle of gravel had been removed.

It'd be hard to do it herself. But it was also hard to sit still and watch his bent head as he concentrated on what he was doing. His fingers were the fingers of a surgeon, she decided. He was skilled and careful and…kind?

He unnerved her. She didn't understand the emotions he engendered and she wasn't sure that she wanted to.

'Th-thank you,' she murmured as he put a dressing in place over the damaged skin.

He smiled up at her. 'Think nothing of it, ma'am. I owe you one.'

'Why?'

'I disparaged your dog.'

'Penelope's Michael's dog,' she said before she could help herself, and he gave a rueful little smile.

'So she is. But isn't there something in the wedding vows that says with all your worldly goods? Doesn't that include Afghan hounds?'

Hugo still thought she was married to Michael. She stared down at the band of gold on her left hand and gave a twisted smile. Married. To Michael. Ha!

But it wasn't the time or the place to disillusion him. What was the point?

Besides, biscuits and cheese weren't nearly enough.

'We need to move on,' she murmured, and he cast her a look that was curiously questioning. And curiously understanding.

'Fine,' he said, and he let his fingers stay on the dressing on her knee for just a fraction of a moment longer than he had to. Long enough to impart...what? Comfort? Understanding? She didn't know.

'Fine,' he told her. 'Let's move on.'

They checked on Kim first. Rachel's stomach couldn't get any louder than it already was, and when Hugo suggested it she agreed. There were some things still more important than food, and seeing Kim safely asleep was one of them.

'She woke a couple of hours back,' Hugo told her. 'But she went back to sleep almost immediately.'

Her body would be so shocked that she'd sleep for days, Rachel thought, and she was sleeping soundly now. Kim's mother was by her side, sitting holding her hand. Doing nothing. She was simply watching.

It was enough.

'Kim shows every sign that she'll be fine,' Hugo told the woman as Rachel watched from the doorway. He lifted the base of Kim's bedsheet to reveal two sets of very pink toes. 'Her circulation's almost back to normal. She's on maximum intravenous antibiotics. Her obs are great. She looks as if she's going to have very little permanent damage. We'll do more nerve tests in the morning but she wiggled everything when she woke and had full sensation. Your husband was watching. Did he tell you?'

'He did.' Mrs Sanderson's face creased in fierce concentration. Concentrating on control. 'I was home getting some things for her when she woke.' Her fragile control broke and her voice choked on a sob. 'I shouldn't have left...'

'Kim needed her things.'

'I mean... I shouldn't have left her at the showgrounds. She wanted to show Knickers. If I'd thought the Jeffreys could be stupid enough to let their dog off the lead... I just didn't realise...how easy it is to lose someone. We came so close.'

'But not close enough,' Hugo said gently, his hand on the woman's shoulder. 'She'll be fine.' He smiled down into her tearful face. 'Tell me how Knickers is.'

It was the right thing to ask. It made the terror recede. The woman gulped and gave him a watery smile. 'Knickers is good.' She took a big breath and searched for calm. She'd been to the brink, Rachel realised. This day would live with her for ever. 'The vet says he'll be OK, though my husband is saying it'll cost more to have Knickers fixed than Kim. We can't claim a cocker spaniel's expenses through medical insurance.'

Hugo grinned. 'See? I'm cheap at half the price.' He smiled, a comfort smile Rachel was starting to recognise. 'Now, what about you going home and getting some rest? We've sedated Kim fairly heavily so I'd be surprised if she woke before morning.'

'I might just watch for a little more,' the woman whispered. 'If it's OK. I just want to watch…'

She just wanted to watch her breathing, Rachel thought. She knew. To sit there and watch a chest rise and fall…

She bit her lip and Hugo turned and saw.

He thought it was the hunger, though. He must do. There was surely no other reason for it. She could see she had him confused and she fought to remove her expression. The stillness of her face…

'I need to take our Dr Harper for a feed,' he told Mrs Sanderson. 'We'll leave you to your vigil. But don't exhaust yourself. Kim will need you in the morning, if only to prevent all her friends from visiting in the first five minutes. Keep up your strength.'

'I will.' The woman smiled through tears. 'Thank you both. We were so lucky…'

* * *

'We *were* really lucky,' Hugo said as they headed out to the parking lot together. 'We were hugely lucky to have you here to help us. We still are.'

Rachel said nothing at all.

The local hall was where the action was. It was set a block back from the main street, but even so Rachel wondered how she could have missed it when she and Penelope had walked into town. Hugo turned the corner and bright lights shone out through open doors. Even at midnight there were dozens of cars parked outside and people were spilling out onto the pavement.

'So this is Cowral Bay's night life,' she said faintly, and Hugo grinned.

'It doesn't get any better than this. Come and meet Cowral. Oh, and I'd take a deep breath if I were you. I suspect you've been voted an honorary local now, like it or not.'

She had. From the moment she walked in the door she was welcomed as a friend. A lifesaver. She'd treated the firemen and she'd treated Kim.

Now she could tell why the pavilion had been locked and darkened—why the town itself had seemed abandoned. Everyone was here. Doris Keen was busy making sandwiches but when she saw Rachel she dropped what she was doing and came forward, her arms outstretched.

'Oh, my dear, we were that worried. We didn't know where you'd got to. We assumed you'd gone home but then Charlie found your husband's car and it was still locked. We searched, but then the fire brigade boys came in and they said you'd gone back to the hospital and you've been working so hard...'

Everyone was assuming Michael was her husband, Rachel thought. She'd been with him. She wore a wedding ring.

It didn't matter. Let them.

She tried to think of Michael with some degree of caring. Had he managed to save Hubert Witherspoon? She didn't know and she didn't much mind. For a moment she almost felt it in her to be sorry for him. He'd left and he'd missed out on…this. This hubbub of caring.

Penelope.

The dog flashed back into her mind and she gave a guilty start. Her dog… Michael's dog was back at the hospital. She half turned, but Hugo was before her.

'Our hospital orderly has taken Penelope home for the night,' he told her. 'Jake's wife has a poodle. We figured they'd get on fine.'

What was it with this man? He had the ability to read what she was thinking almost as she thought it. The feeling was really, really unnerving.

'This lady's a real champion,' someone said behind her, and she recognised one of the men who'd been on the fire truck. There were scores of firefighters here. This must be their refuelling station before they went back to the fire or turned in for the night.

'She's a hungry real champion,' Hugo said from behind her. His hand was on her shoulder and for some reason it was a huge support. His warmth gave her shaking legs strength. Somehow his presence made this welcome feel real—as if she was part of all this.

But it wasn't real, she told herself a little bit desperately. It was an illusion. She was most definitely not a part of this. She cast Hugo an unsure glance and pulled away from under his hand.

But then she missed it when he released her. She missed…the contact? The link?

What?

'Daddy!' a voice yelled out from the other side of the

hall and a tousle-headed, pyjama-clad Toby came bounding through the crowd of locals to greet him. Hugo reached out and caught him, swinging him high in the air.

'Tobes. Why aren't you in bed?'

'Mrs Partridge made me have an afternoon sleep,' Toby said, with all the indignation of a small man whose person has been significantly violated. 'She said we'd all had a nasty shock and she needed a lie-down, too. So I went to sleep. And now I'm wide awake and Mrs Partridge's helping me make lamingtons for the firefighters to eat tomorrow. Can we stay for a while, Daddy?'

'Yes, we can,' he told him, hugging him close. 'Far be it from me to interfere with lamington-making. And we need to wait for Dr Harper to be fed.'

'Why?'

'Because we're taking her home to stay with us.'

To stay with them? He had to be kidding.

He wasn't. 'There's nowhere else.'

Full to the brim of Irish stew, fresh bread rolls and Toby's magnificent lamingtons, Rachel was tucked into Hugo's capacious car with as much room for argument as if she'd been a parcel.

'But why?'

'You've already discovered the motel's full. There's a couple of beds at the hospital but we need them. While this fire's burning I want all resources left free for emergencies. Toby and I have a big house at the rear of the hospital and there's two spare bedrooms.'

'But your wife…'

'I'm a widower,' he said bluntly. 'But I'm trustworthy.' He put on his most trustworthy smile and she had to smile.

'No, but—'

'Exactly. No buts. Can you think of anywhere better?' He

smiled across at her and his smile had her insides doing strange things. Very strange things indeed. This was no trustworthy smile. It looked exactly the opposite.

But he was still speaking. She had to concentrate. 'There's no women's refuge to be had,' he was saying. 'Despite the rumours. The dog pavilion's closed for the night and something tells me you weren't very comfortable there last night anyway. And the park benches are exceedingly hard. So it's us or nothing.'

'We really want you to stay,' Toby announced from the back seat. 'Me and Digger like you. Even though your dress looks funny.'

'Gee, thanks.' She fingered the Crimplene and wondered how it was that the Crimplene was the least odd thing in the succession of things that had happened to her today.

'We'll do something about that tomorrow,' Hugo announced. 'But for now, we'd be very pleased if you took up our offer of accommodation, Dr Harper. What about it?'

What about it? There was only one answer to that. She had no choice.

'Yes, please,' she said, and decided then and there that arguing was out of the question.

Things were entirely out of her hands.

CHAPTER FOUR

THE house they took her to was a big old timber home in the same grounds as the hospital. It had wide verandas all around and a garden that in the dim light cast by the hospital nightlights looked overgrown and rambling. Digger was lying on the front steps. When they arrived he rushed down to greet them, his whole body quivering in delight. Hugo pushed open the front door, Rachel walked inside as he followed, carrying Toby—and she stopped still in astonishment.

This wasn't a home. It was an artwork.

A magnificent artwork.

Like something out of *Vogue*, it had been furnished with exquisite taste. In rich reds and golds, every piece of furnishing was richly ornate and highly decorative. The floor was sleekly polished with gorgeous Persian rugs scattered at artistic intervals. There were elegant pieces of sculpture, carefully placed. The settees and chairs were colour coordinated with dainty matching cushions, artfully arranged. Heavy brocade curtains were held back, looped and looped again with vast gold tassels that hung to the floor.

Good grief!

This wasn't a doctor's residence. It wasn't a child's residence.

It was frankly…scary.

But Hugo seemed oblivious, both to his surroundings and to her reaction. 'Toby, would you show Dr Harper where she'll sleep?' he asked. 'I'll put the coffee on.' He disappeared in the direction of the kitchen while Toby towed her through to the back of the house.

The further she went the more awful it became.

'This room's where my daddy sleeps and this is where Digger and I sleep,' Toby told her, and Rachel had glimpses of two rooms with the same amazing furnishings. He towed her further. 'You can have this room or this room.'

It made no difference which. Gorgeous brocade beds with hugely rich furnishings. Huge gold bows of something like velvet with threads of something shining and metallic hung at each corner of the bed. The beds looked like they took half an hour of intense concentration and a degree in interior design to make each morning!

Ugh.

'Do you and your daddy like…um…really decorated houses?' she asked, as Toby stood and waited for her verdict.

His small face furrowed in concentration. 'Why?'

'Your whole house is sort of…frilly. And red. And gold. You guys must really like red and gold, huh?'

'I like purple,' Toby told her.

'So Daddy likes red and gold?'

'I think he likes blue.' Toby considered some more. 'Or maybe yellow. Mr Addington at the bank has a really yellow car and whenever my dad sees it he whistles and says what a beauty.'

'So why is your house red and gold?'

'My mummy decorated the house,' Toby told her. 'My mummy died just after I was born. Daddy was really sad.'

'I guess he would be.' Rachel's face softened. 'Losing your mummy would be really hard.'

'Yeah, but I didn't know her,' Toby said with the blunt pragmatism of a six-year-old. 'My daddy says Aunty Christine looks like her. The photos are a bit the same. And

Aunty Christine loves this house. She comes in here and looks at it and cries.'

Oh, great...

'Aunty Christine says Digger shouldn't come into the house because he messes it up but Daddy said he put his foot down over that, whatever that means,' Toby told her. 'And I want a Darth Vader poster on my bedroom wall 'cos Daddy and I love that movie, but Aunty Christine says my mummy would hate it and I mustn't even ask Daddy because it'd make him sad. Do you think it'd make him sad? Or is it something else he'd put his foot down about?'

'Maybe.' This wasn't a conversation she should get drawn into, she decided. Not when she'd known these people for not much more than two minutes.

There was lots of background here that she didn't understand.

But at least she had a bed, she decided, brightening. An amazing bed. She'd had a truly excellent meal. She could put up with a little red and gold opulence.

She sat down on the bed. It gave under her weight. She gave a tentative bounce and the bed bounced back.

The symmetry of the covers was ruined.

Great.

'Do you do much bouncing?' she asked Toby, and he looked like he didn't know what she was talking about.

'You ruin the covers if you bounce,' he told her. 'Aunty Christine says so. She says don't move things. Don't touch. She says Mummy would have everything perfect.'

Rachel's eyes widened. What an extraordinary statement. 'But...bouncing's fun. I'm sure your mummy would want you to have fun.'

'Aunty Christine would growl at me if I bounced on my bed.'

'Would she growl at you if you bounced on mine?'

Toby thought about it. Deeply. 'I guess she wouldn't,' he said at last. 'You're a grown-up. She couldn't growl at you.'

'I'd like to see her try.' She'd never met the unknown Aunt Christine but already she held her in aversion. And Hugo... What had they created? A shrine to a dead wife and sister when it should be a home.

She knew—who better?—that life was to be lived by the living. For the living. Not for the dead.

It could all be taken away so quickly...

Enough. She bounced again. And smiled at Toby and moved along so that there was room beside her. 'Want to try?

'Yes,' Toby said, and went to join her.

They bounced.

Digger, watching from the doorway, ventured further in, looking as stunned as it was possible for a goofy dog to look.

They continued to bounce.

Digger started to bark and Toby giggled and bounced higher.

It was great. Stupid but great.

It had been one heck of a day. Rachel's emotions had been pushed to the limit. She didn't know what she was doing here. She didn't have a clue what was happening to her, but for now...for this minute there was just one crazy time, a tousle-headed child who looked as if he didn't get enough laughter in his life and Rachel. And Rachel knew she definitely needed more laughter. More bouncing.

If the springs broke, she'd pay for them, she decided. If the tassels frayed. If the gilt was tarnished. Some things just had to be done, and they had to be done now. She had hold of Toby's hands and they were bouncing in unison as Digger barked a crazy accompaniment on the side.

'What on earth...?'

She looked over to the doorway. Hugo was watching them. Stunned. 'What on earth do you think you're doing?'

She refused to give up the moment. Not yet. She'd had a very big day and so had Toby. A vision of Toby's face as he'd watched them work on Kim came back to her. It was too much horror for a six-year-old to be put to bed with. He needed to sleep with bouncing.

'We're bouncing, Dr McInnes,' she told him, then gripped Toby's hands tighter and bounced again. 'Care to join us?'

'You'll break the bedsprings.'

'I'll pay for them,' she said nobly. 'I'm donating one set of bedsprings to the common good. I need a bounce and so does Toby. I'm sure you do, too.'

'I wouldn't fit,' he said faintly, and she grinned.

'That's what you get for showing your guest to a room with a single bed.'

'Daddy's got a bigger bed,' Toby volunteered, mid-bounce. 'Can we can go there?'

Digger barked again as if he thought that was a truly excellent idea.

'My bed's for sleeping in,' Hugo told them, and Rachel grimaced.

'How boring.'

'The kettle's boiled. Do you want a drink?'

Rachel considered. She bounced a couple of times and looked down at Toby. He bounced with her and met her look—co-conspirators. Co-bouncers. 'Do we want a drink, Toby?'

'I'd like some hot chocolate,' he told her, and bounced again.

'That sounds good.' Another bounce. 'Maybe we could stop and bounce again tomorrow night.'

'Are you staying for two nights?'

She cast a sideways glance at Hugo and bounced a bit more. 'I may,' she told him. 'If I'm not kicked out because of my bouncing habits. I think I'm needed.'

'Because of the fire?' Toby asked, and she nodded.

'Because of the fire. And because…maybe because you guys could do with a bit of bouncing. Like me.'

What was happening here?

Hugo prepared three mugs of hot chocolate and listened to their laughter. He'd backed out of the room fast.

Why?

He didn't know. Confusion, he thought. He was definitely confused. The sight of one crazy doctor, gorgeous in her borrowed Crimplene, holding his little son and bouncing as if she were six years old, too…

Confusion summed it up, he thought. She was like no one he'd ever met.

She was…gorgeous?

She was also married. She was wearing a band of gold very definitely on the third finger of her left hand. She was attached to a creep called Michael.

How attached?

Married attached.

But, then…he wore a wedding band as well.

Why?

Habit, he guessed. Beth had been dead for almost six years now.

So why did he keep wearing the ring?

The vision of Christine came into his head. Beth's older sister. Christine, who came in every day and cared for Toby, fussed over this house, made sure Toby had a memory of his mother.

Christine would marry him. He knew that. She was just waiting for him to move on from her sister.

So he wore a wedding ring.

'It's time you got over it,' Christine had told him, but he wasn't ready. He hadn't been ready to marry Beth. He hadn't wanted to marry anyone.

The memory of his parents' loveless marriage was always there—his mother, cool and calculating, with eyes only for things of monetary value, and his father who'd had eyes only for women he could bed. He himself had been raised to be self-contained, aloof and indifferent, and only Toby had ever been able to get under his skin.

The thought of Rachel came back into his vision. Bouncing. Christine would never bounce. Not in a fit.

Neither would Beth, his ex-wife, have bounced. Neither would his mother.

Rachel was…different.

But Rachel had a husband. He thought back to the silver-haired cardiologist he'd met so briefly. The man might be odious, but he was obviously an extremely wealthy and well-connected doctor, and they were married. So Rachel might be bouncing in his spare bedroom with his small son but she had a husband and an Afghan hound and a life back in the city.

So stop thinking of her like…what?

Like his father thought of women?

No. It wasn't like that. This was something he had never felt before—in truth, he'd never known he could feel this way. Ever. But he was certainly feeling, and the problem was—he couldn't stop to save himself.

The hot chocolate was excellent. Exhausted, glowing with exertion from their bouncing, Rachel and Toby enjoyed it equally. Hugo watched them as he'd watch two kids with their play lunch, and Rachel looked up and caught his eye and said, 'What?'

'What do you mean—what?'

'What are you grinning at?'

'I was just thinking you and Toby look of an age.'

'Toby is very mature for six.' She set her mug down on the table and rose to her feet, which all of a sudden didn't feel too steady. It had been a roller-coaster of a day and she was rolling downward to sleep. 'And I'm sure it's Toby's and my bedtime. Toby had an afternoon nap. I didn't even have a nap last night.'

'Why not?'

'It'd take far too long to explain,' she said with dignity. She eyed him with indecision. 'I suppose you wouldn't happen to have a spare toothbrush, would you? My gear's still at the showgrounds.'

'Not only a toothbrush.' He grinned. 'While you and Toby were bouncing I made you up a sleeping kit. One pair of pyjamas, slightly large, one brand-new toothbrush and a comb. Everything else you need you'll find in the guest bathroom.'

She swallowed. Heck. It was a small enough gesture, but it was enough. The man was thoughtful.

The man smiled!

The man was seriously gorgeous.

'Goodnight, then,' she said, and there was a distinct tremor in her voice.

His smile died and their eyes met. Something passed between them that was indefinable but it was still…there.

But there was nothing to say. To try and bring it into the open—this thing…

Impossible.

'Goodnight,' he said, and she knew he was thinking no such thing. He was thinking exactly what she was thinking.

Impossible!

*   *   *

What was it with her?

Hugo stood and watched while Rachel walked away from him down the corridor to her bedroom. Her door closed behind her but he stood and watched for a very long time.

What was it?

'Dottie?'

'My dear, why are you ringing at this time of night?'

'I'm checking.' Rachel was tucked into her opulent bed, her cellphone resting on her pillow. 'I just need… Dottie, I need to know…'

'You know he's just the same. He always will be just the same, whether you're here or not. Now, are you somewhere nice with that nice young man?'

'I…' Rachel bit her lip. That nice young man.

Maybe she could apply the adjective to Toby.

'Yes,' she said. 'Yes, I am.'

'Has he taken you somewhere gorgeous?'

She smiled at that. This, at least, was an easy question. 'It's all red and gold brocade,' she whispered. 'And incredibly luxurious. Dottie, you should see the bed.'

There was a moment's silence. And then Dottie spoke again, deeply satisfied.

'Then why are you wasting time on the phone talking about it?' she demanded. 'You put your phone down this minute and go and make the most of it.'

Make the most of it? That was a joke.

Rachel put the phone down and pulled up her covers but in the end she did make the most of it. Or she did what she most needed to do.

She slept.

Digger was barking.

Rachel surfaced to sunlight streaming in over her bed.

She blinked, trying to figure out just where she was. Memory came flooding back. She stretched out in her too-big pyjamas and thought this wasn't such a bad place to live if you took away the brocade. And the tassels. And the particularly ghastly cupids staring dotingly down from the mantelpiece.

Her bedroom was facing east. She'd hauled back the dreadful crimson drapes the night before and now she could see right out to the ocean beyond. Why the bedroom had drapes she didn't know, unless the local cows were nosy. There were cows in the paddock beyond the house, the sea was beyond the cows and beyond the sea was the horizon. A smoky haze was filtering the light but it still looked great.

Her apartment at the hospital looked out at a brick wall.

Maybe she could move to the country when Craig...

Yeah, right. Get a grip.

Craig.

She groped under her bed for her purse, checked the time—it was eight o'clock, far later than she usually slept even after huge nights on call!—found her phone and dialled home. Some things were automatic.

But some things weren't needed. Or wanted.

'What are you doing, ringing again?' Dorothy sounded cross that she'd contacted her. 'I told you not to and I meant it. Rachel, leave it be. I can't tell you how delighted we are that you're having a good time.'

'But Craig?'

There was silence. Then: 'You know very well how Craig is, dear. I told you. Lewis popped in before breakfast and he's stable. As he always is. Rachel, it's no use ringing.'

'But you will let me know...'

'Rachel, love, nothing's going to change and you know it. You go back to whatever it is you're doing,' her mother-in-law said gently. 'Stop ringing. Move on. Get yourself a life.'

A life. Right. Dorothy thought she was having a nice romantic time.

She looked down at herself, dressed in what she guessed were Hugo's spare pyjamas. Blue and yellow stripes. Very fetching.

She looked at the bedside chair where Doris's Crimplene lay waiting.

'Which?' she said to herself. 'Romantic choice, eh? Which would Cinderella wear, and where's my fairy god-mother when I need her?'

Hugo and Toby and the plump, round-faced lady she'd seen taking care of Toby yesterday were all having breakfast. Oh, and Digger. The lady was just setting down a plate of scraps under the table. This was clearly doggy heaven.

It was Rachel heaven. She sniffed. Bacon. Coffee. Toast.

Some things were irresistible. She hitched up her pyjamas and hiked right in.

'Hi,' she said, and tried not to look self-conscious.

'Hi,' said Toby, while the lady and Hugo just looked.

'No comment is required,' she told them. She glared at Hugo—at the lurking laughter she could see behind his eyes. 'Don't even think about it.' She held out her hand to the bacon lady, while the other still clutched her waist. 'I'm Rachel.'

'I'm Myra Partridge,' the lady told her, taking her hand and gripping it with warmth and real friendliness. She eyed Rachel's outfit in concern. 'They're not the doctor's pyjamas?'

'I have no idea,' she told her. 'They're the ones the doctor kindly gave me last night. All I know is that they're not this doctor's pyjamas. They're threatening to slide, but I've decided that they still look better on me than Doris Keen's frock does.'

'Oh, my dear…' Myra's lips twitched. She was in her late fifties, Rachel guessed, with eyes that said she smiled most of the time. She reached into a kitchen drawer and proffered a safety pin—which Rachel accepted with real gratitude. 'I saw you in Doris's frock last night. Doris rang a while back.'

'If she wants her frock back, she's welcome to it.' Rachel thought about it. 'Though she might want to come and get it. I can't see myself hiking over to her place in these.'

'Sit yourself down.' They were all smiling now as she stuck the safety pin in place—all three of them. The kitchen felt great. Here the opulence and over-decoration were toned down by the sheer domesticity of cooking and the dog under the table and smiling people. There were pots and pans and…

'Pancakes?' Rachel said faintly.

'I thought you'd all be hungry.' Myra beamed. 'The doctor's been out since dawn.'

'Has he?' Rachel's smile slipped. She looked across the table at Hugo. 'Problems?'

'Kim's running a fever. Not too bad. I'm hoping it's nothing. I've upped the antibiotics to maximum. And a couple of the fire crews have been working through the night. I checked them as they came in.'

'He'd be doing something else if it wasn't Kim and the fire crews,' Myra said comfortably. 'He's always gone at dawn. I come in and look after the wee one…'

'Until Aunty Christine comes in and takes me to school,' Toby told her. 'Mrs Partridge would take me to school and I want her to, but Aunty Christine makes Dad let her.'

She wasn't buying into any family argument. Not yet. 'Well, lucky you to have two ladies to escort you.' She wriggled herself around in her pyjamas, testing the security of the pin. She let go the waist and did a little test jump—her hands hovering just in case, while Hugo, Toby, Myra and Digger looked on, fascinated. They were doomed to disappointment. The safety pin held. She sat herself down and reached for a pancake, deeply satisfied. 'You were going to wake me up for some of these, right?'

Hugo was looking at her with a very strange expression. 'Um…right.'

'I wanted to wake you up hours ago,' Toby announced. 'But Daddy wouldn't let me.'

'You have a very kind daddy.' Rachel beamed. 'Just as long as he lets me share his pancakes and his bacon and coffee. Very kind indeed.'

Clothes. That was the most important thing.

'Doris dropped your bag off an hour ago,' Myra told her. 'But she's kept your clothes. There's stains…'

'I don't want to know about them,' Rachel said firmly, thinking about the last time she'd seen them and deciding if she never saw them again it'd be too soon. 'There's nothing wrong with Crimplene and flannelette.'

'Digger saved your bra,' Toby told her, and she faltered. Her bra. The last time she'd seen that had been…

Whoops!

'Flannelette and Crimplene and lacy black bras are hardly professional,' Hugo told her, and Rachel managed a sickly sort of smile.

'Um…no. Not your white-coated doctor image, huh?'

'No,' he said faintly, and her grin widened. Hey, it wasn't he who was doing the discomposing. It was suddenly Hugo who was discomposed. She had Hugo McInnes out of his comfort zone, which felt…good.

Definitely good, she decided. He made her discomposed. It was nice to have him a little discomposed in return.

But he was about to discompose her again. 'I think we have the problem sorted,' he told her.

'Mmm?' She was into a mouthful of bacon. Yesterday's hunger was still fresh enough to make her really appreciate her food and this was seriously good.

'Christine's bringing you some clothes.'

She thought about it. 'Christine.' She looked at Toby. 'Red and gold Christine?'

They all knew what she meant. There were three smiles. But Hugo was rising, pushing back his coffee-cup. 'She's very good. I don't know where we'd be without her. And she's not red and gold at all. She has a style all her own.' He glanced at his watch. 'She should be here in a few minutes to take Toby to school. I need to do a house call. If it's OK with you, Rachel, I'll collect you in an hour and take you out to our nursing home. I was hoping you might be able to help.'

He paused as if what he was asking was an impertinence, but she wasn't in the mood for worrying over impertinence.

'Of course I'll help. If I'm trapped here I may as well be useful. But how?'

'The fires are worsening.' He motioned to the window and the haze between there and the sea seem to be thicker. 'They're not threatening the town yet but the crews are working hard to keep it like that. And most of the crews are made up of volunteers with differing levels of fitness—as well as differing levels of common sense. There are lots of medical problems. I need to go up to the ridge.'

'So you'd like me to do the coughs and colds and the like while you do the hero stuff?'

'Would you?'

'Of course I would.' She grinned at him. There was something about this man that made her want to smile—even when she was offering to do his mundane work for him while he did the exciting stuff. 'Though I guess that means I don't get to drive fire trucks any more.'

His smile matched hers. 'I heard about your fire-truck driving. Very impressive. But still...' His eyes smiled at her—linking them—warming parts of her she hadn't known were cold. Crazy. But...nice? 'You're hardly dressed for fire-truck duty.'

She looked down at her pyjamas and pouted. 'What's wrong with these? I reckon I'd look pretty snappy behind the wheel of a fire truck in flannelette pyjamas.'

'Your safety pin would never hold.' He chuckled, and the strange link was broken. For now. 'OK. Let's negotiate the duty roster when we're organised. When you're wearing something a bit more doctor-like. Meanwhile, I have to go. Myra, can you—?'

He was interrupted in mid-sentence. The back door swung wide—and in walked Christine.

It wasn't hard to pick her. Rachel looked up from her bacon and she knew straight away who this had to be.

The lady was seriously lovely. She also wasn't decorated at all. She didn't need to be. What had Hugo said? 'She has a style all her own.'

She certainly did.

She was tall, with flame-coloured hair swept up into a sleek knot, the hair itself seeming to tug the flawless complexion free of any lines.

No lines would dare come near this woman. She was wearing cropped black pants to calf length, a tiny white top, strappy black sandals and a silver bracelet that must have cost a fortune.

She looked as if she belonged in an inner-city art gallery,

Rachel thought, with only one very fast rueful glance down at her pyjamas. She thought back to the people she'd seen yesterday at the Cowral show. This woman didn't fit.

'Hello, all.' The woman's greeting was bright and warm. She smiled straight at Hugo, though, Rachel noticed, and Toby didn't look up from his breakfast. 'Are you ready, Toby?'

You can see he's still eating his breakfast, Rachel thought, but she didn't say so. The question seemed to be rhetorical. Christine had dropped a carry bag on the floor and was reaching for the coffee-pot. 'Heaven. You make the best coffee, Hugo.'

'Harrumph.' Myra rose and stumped over to the sink and Rachel wondered who had made the coffee. By the expression on Myra's face it wasn't hard to guess. Maybe it didn't matter, though. Christine had moved on.

'You're the new doctor?' Christine sank into the chair Myra had just left, as if it was her right, and turned her attention to Rachel. 'So you're Rachel. I've heard all about you.' She motioned to the bag. 'There are some clothes I purchased for you from our local discount store. I hope they're what you want, Hugo?'

They're what Hugo wanted?

Rachel raised her brows at Hugo and he attempted a smile. He looked a bit uncomfortable.

'I phoned Christine and told her you were in trouble.'

'Who, me?' Rachel tried hard to sound nonchalant. 'I like pyjamas.' Discount store, hey? Obviously she'd been categorised by Crimplene. She swallowed her last piece of pancake and smiled at all of them.

Discount store.

Maybe she should put that aside. There were undercurrents here that she clearly didn't understand. Undercurrents that were maybe more important than her pride.

Toby was concentrating fiercely on his pancake and wasn't looking at anyone. Myra was looking angry. What was going on?

It didn't matter. This wasn't her place and these people had nothing to do with her. In a couple of days the fires would die down and she'd be out of here.

'The clothes are all here.' Christine swept a manicured hand at her bag and smiled at Hugo, and Rachel thought, Unconcerned or not, I'm with Toby here. His little nose was practically in his toast.

But she knew her manners. 'Thank you, Christine,' she told her. 'Have you bought them? How much do I owe you?'

'I'll pay,' Hugo said, but Christine put a hand sweetly on his arm.

'It's fine, dear. The Mathesons, who run the discount store, know you're stuck. They won't charge you.'

Hugo was stuck?

Gee, she was having fun here, Rachel thought—or she didn't think.

She rose and lifted Christine's obnoxious bag. She hated it already, even though she hadn't opened it. 'I'll pick up my bill from...who did you say? Mathesons? If I really need this,' she told them. 'Otherwise I'll return it. Thank you anyway, Christine. Now, if you'll excuse me...'

She huffed at the lot of them. Toby looked up at her and she caught the six-year-old's eye and gave him a tiny sideways wink.

Then she sailed from the room with as much dignity as a girl in too-big pyjamas could muster.

'They're horrible.'

They were all gone—Toby and Hugo and Christine. Christine to take Toby to school and Hugo to do his house call. Rachel peered out into the kitchen where Myra was washing the dishes. The housekeeper turned and Rachel looked at her with despair in her eyes.

'I can't wear these.'

'Sorry?' The housekeeper wiped her hands on the dish-cloth and looked Rachel up and down. Rachel was wearing Doris's Crimplene again.

'Look!'

She held up a pair of black trousers. Plain. Dead plain. Voluminous with a heavy vinyl belt. She held up a neat white cotton blouse. Another identical blouse. A plain black cardigan. Black flat-soled sandals.

'At least Doris's Crimplene has flowers on,' she wailed. 'And Hugo's pyjamas have stripes. Myra, I may be stuck here, but these are awful.'

'Christine only wears black and white,' Myra said dubiously, coming forward and taking the offending garments away from her. 'Only…'

'Only Christine's clothes are beautifully cut and really, really stylish and these clothes are built to fit anyone! Anyone at all. Or no one. These are burial clothes, Myra.'

Myra cast her another dubious glance. 'You don't think maybe you're going over the top here?'

'No.' Rachel's chin jutted. 'I may be stuck here but I refuse to look like Christine's welfare case while I'm here.'

'You don't wear black, huh?'

'No way.' It was the one thing she had in life—her clothes. She wore happy clothes, the sort of clothes that'd make Craig smile if he…

No. She wasn't going down that road, but she didn't wear black. Ever.

'You're wearing pink,' she told Myra, and if she sounded a bit like a sulky teenager she couldn't help it.

But Myra was smiling. 'Tell you what. I've finished the

dishes,' she told her. 'I'm officially off duty until Toby comes home from school. We have an hour before Dr McInnes returns.'

'So?'

Myra glanced at her watch. 'It's not yet nine and Eileen Sanderson doesn't usually open until ten. But if it's for you...'

'Eileen Sanderson?'

'Kim's mum.'

'Oh, no. I can't—'

'She owns Cowral Bay's only decent dress shop and it's great. Expensive but good.'

'But she'll be with Kim.'

'She's home. I saw Brian, her husband, swap shifts with her a couple of hours ago as I was coming here and she lives next door to the store.'

'But she'll be asleep.'

'Not Eileen.'

'I can't—'

'Rachel, you saved her daughter's life,' Myra told her. 'You helped the firefighters last night. There's not a soul in Cowral Bay who wouldn't drop everything to help you right now.' She frowned and looked again at the black, shapeless trousers. 'Except maybe Christine.' And she tossed her dish-cloth aside with a determined throw, grasped Rachel by the hand and towed her out to her car.

Hugo drove home an hour later, his thoughts overwhelmed with what lay ahead.

The fire was worse. The forecast was for a strong north-east wind, which would bring the fire down from the ridge. Already the town was shrouded by a pall of smoke so heavy Hugo had to put on his headlights.

There'd be heat exhaustion as well as fire-related injuries, he thought grimly. It was already scorchingly hot. If the fire grew worse... If there were emergencies...

He needed back-up.

He was set up here as a single doctor. Usually—well, sometimes—one doctor was enough. In a sleepy fishing village there was no need for a huge medical presence. Few doctors wanted to practise in such a remote area and the swell of campers during summer wasn't enough to tempt medics wanting a high income.

Normally Hugo didn't mind working alone—he even liked it—but his radio was telling him a quarter of the state was under threat from fire. That meant relief medical teams wouldn't be forthcoming even in an emergency. There was only him—but now at least there was Rachel as well.

But if the road cleared just for a few hours...

She'd be out of here, he thought grimly. She had a husband and the world's stupidest dog and a city career. She was a fine doctor—hell, she had the skills he desperately needed in a partner—but she'd be out of here.

The road was still cut, though, he thought, and as far he could see that was the only bright spot on his horizon. He had a captive worker and she'd said she'd work.

A captive worker...

He thought of Rachel as he'd last seen her. In those crazy pyjamas. His mouth twitched and his bleakness lifted a little. She was here. She had said she'd work. Now, as long as Christine had fitted her out in some sensible clothes...

He pulled into the driveway, looked down at the list of things he still had to do this morning and went to find his colleague.

He walked through the screen door and stopped dead.

Good grief!

Rachel was sitting at the kitchen table, helping Myra pod peas. She'd obviously reclaimed Penelope. Penelope and

Digger were lying side by side under the table looking extraordinarily pleased with each other, but that wasn't where Hugo's attention was caught and held.

Rachel was only five-four or so—a good eight inches shorter than he was—but what she lacked in height she made up for in impact. This morning in his pyjamas she'd looked amazing. But now...

She was wearing bright yellow leggings that stopped at mid-calf, and a white overshirt that looked as if it had been splashed by daubs of yellow paint. Her shirt was rolled up, businesslike, but there was nothing businesslike in the way it was unbuttoned to show enough cleavage to be interesting. Very interesting! So interesting he could hardly take his eyes away.

What else? He could scarcely take her in. Apart from the cleavage... Her riot of shining brown curls was caught back with a wide yellow ribbon and her feet were ensconced in gold and white trainers.

'Christine never gave you those clothes,' he said faintly, and she chuckled.

'Good guess. Mrs Sanderson's a darling and she has such taste. I returned the clothes Christine brought me. I'm very grateful but they just weren't me.' She held up a shoe and admired it. 'And gold and white trainers...how practical are these?'

'Very practical,' he said weakly, and she grinned. She rose and looked expectantly out to the car.

'Are we heading out to the nursing home now?'

'You're not wearing that outfit to the nursing home?'

'Why ever not?'

'I'm thinking of their hearts. I don't think I'm carrying enough anginine,' he said, and she chuckled again. She had the nicest chuckle...

'You're telling me the oldies won't like my clothes?'

'I have no idea,' he managed. 'I do know they'll neve
have seen anything like it in their lives.' He looked dow
at her amazing shoes. 'You don't think gold and white i
this ash might be just a little impractical?'

'They'll wash. I'm not putting Doris's sandals back o
for quids. They may be sensible but I don't do sensible.'

'So I see.'

The oldies not only loved Rachel's clothes—they love
Rachel.

In this heat and smoke-filled atmosphere, the ills of
group of sixty frail retirees could be depended on to keep
Hugo busy for half a day, but only a couple of problem
were serious. Hugo expected to do the tricky stuff himsel
while Rachel took a routine clinic, but Rachel had no soone
been introduced to the sitting room in general, and the nurs
in charge in particular, than she balked.

'Tell me why you're staying?'

'I have a couple of bed-bound patients I'll check befor
I go.'

'You're telling me that I can't check them? That you
don't think I'm competent?'

'No, but—'

'Then you're not needed anywhere else?'

'Of course he is.' Don, the nursing-home charge nurse,
beefy, bearded giant, was clearly amused by the strange ten
sion between the two. And the way Hugo kept glancing a
his colleague as if he couldn't believe his eyes. 'I've had
call from the hospital already saying there's another coupl
of firefighters need looking at, and they've just admitte
Harry Peters's kid, who fell off the back of the fire truc
and broke his arm. They want you back there, Hugo.'

'I can't just leave you here,' Hugo said, frowning at th
jonquil-yellow apparition in front of him.

'Why not?' The jonquil-yellow apparition raised herself up on her jonquil-yellow toes and glared. 'Are you saying you're a better doctor than I am?'

'No, but—'

'Then take me to the patients you're worried about, talk me through what needs to be done and then get out of here. No more buts. You're wasting time, Dr McInnes.'

Wasting time?

No one had ever accused Hugo McInnes of wasting time. Ever. It was all he could do not to gasp.

'Go on, then.' Don was clearly intrigued and enjoying himself. 'What are you waiting for, Hugo?'

He hardly knew.

CHAPTER FIVE

IT WAS harder work than she'd thought it would be.

Rachel had been working in an emergency department for the last four years, coping with emergencies. These weren't emergencies. She had to scour her brain for the things she'd learned in basic training—how to dress and treat leg ulcers, how to look after a man who was suffering long-term effects of the cortisone he'd taken after suffering rheumatoid arthritis for forty years, how to ease the passing of an old lady—ninety-eight, her bed card said, but she was still able to smile and grasp Rachel's hand in greeting—a lady who might only have days left to live.

Rachel had asked Hugo to let her do this, so he had left her to it. She hadn't realised until he'd gone that it had been quite an act of faith. Of trust.

'I'll come back and collect you at lunchtime,' he'd told her, and had gone off to see to his town patients and his firefighters. He was needed.

So was she. She couldn't think about Hugo. She had enough to concentrate on herself.

But the oldies were lovely. They helped her all the way. Don was at her side, and everyone knew the routine.

'Dr Hugo uses that sort of dressing,' she was told by a patient, the very elderly Mrs Collins, before Don could open his mouth. She cast him a sideways grin and started wrapping Mrs Collins's ulcer with the dressing the old lady had pointed at.

'Do I get the feeling this place would run on its own if we weren't here?' she asked.

'We learn to be self-sufficient,' Don told her. 'There's days when Hugo can't come.'

'When he's on holidays?'

'When there are emergencies in the town he can't come,' Don told her. 'Only then. Our Dr McInnes doesn't do holidays.'

'What, never?'

'He last took a holiday three years ago.' Don bent and helped her adjust the dressing. Mrs Collins, eighty-nine and very, very interested in this yellow doctor, was listening avidly as she was treated. 'I don't think he knows the meaning of the word holiday. Christine takes Toby to New York to visit his grandmother during school holidays—paid for by Hugo—and that's it.'

'It sounds a pretty dreary life.'

'It's a better life now than when he was married,' Don said bluntly. 'Some marriages are the pits.'

Hmm. 'Should you be saying this to me?' Rachel raised her eyebrows at the bearded nurse and Don grinned.

'Nope. But if we can't gossip, what's the use of living? Isn't that right, Mrs Collins?'

'That's dead right.' Sheila Collins's old eyes perused Rachel and suddenly she leaned over and grabbed her hand. She held it up.

'You're married yourself?' she demanded, and Rachel met her look square on.

'Yes.'

'Not separated or anything?'

'No.'

'So when this fire is over and the road's cleared, you'll go back to your husband.'

There was only one answer to that. 'Of course I will.'

The old lady's look was steady. News must travel fast in this town. Everyone was really well informed. Frighteningly well informed. 'They say you were fighting with your husband at the dog show. They say he's a creep and a bully. And he left our Kim for dead.'

'No one here knows my husband,' Rachel said steadily.

'First impressions…'

There were places Rachel wasn't prepared to go. No one needed explanations. 'No one here knows him,' she said again.

'Stay out of her space, Sheila,' Don said sternly. 'Or you just might get iodine on those legs.'

Sheila's eyes narrowed. She stared at Rachel for a moment longer and then gave a cackle of laughter. 'Oh, sure. I guess it'd serve me right if I do. But it's not just me who's curious. She wants to know about our Dr McInnes as much as we want to know about her.'

'Then tell her.' Don was in his fifties or maybe a little older. He looked contented, Rachel thought. He looked like a nurse who'd spent his life caring for people in a small town—and who was content to do so for as long as he could.

The feeling was suddenly…nice. Living in Cowral would be a good life, she thought. She'd never considered country medical practice. Maybe she…

Maybe after…

No.

'Our Dr Hugo made a bad marriage,' Sheila told her, and Rachel forced herself to concentrate. Not that that was very hard. Sheila was right. She really did want to know.

'Why?'

'He didn't have much of a home life, our Doc Hugo,' Sheila said. 'His mother was a right little cow—only after what she could get. She lit out for the city as soon as she could and we never saw her again. But Hugo used to come down here. Old Dr McInnes had been here for as long as anyone can remember, and whenever his mother wanted to get rid of him—which was often—Hugo used to come down to stay. He loved his grandpa. Then the old man had a stroke soon after Hugo qualified as a doctor, and Hugo came for good. I don't think he had much choice. He came because he loved the old man and then he was sort of stuck.'

So he hadn't come through choice…

'He was really unsettled at first.' Don took over the tale then. They were a pair, Rachel thought—the nurse who looked like he'd be more at home on a logging truck than in a nursing home, and the ancient lady whose bright eyes gleamed with intelligence. And…mischief? 'The old man was ill for a couple of years,' Don continued, with only a sideways glance and a twinkle to show he knew exactly what Rachel was thinking. 'Hugo was here, helping him. It must have been a huge shock after practising medicine in Sydney.'

'But then he met Beth,' the old lady chipped in. 'Christine and Beth. They came down here to paint. Their parents were divorced. Their father had a fishing shack here so living was cheap. They had nothing to bless themselves with, but they thought they were the best thing since sliced bread. Their mother has a studio in New York and that's how they dressed—like they'd just walked off the streets of Manhattan. They complained because no one knew how to make decent coffee.'

'They were exotic and they were gorgeous,' Don added. 'They were also really, really expensive. Their paintings were incomprehensible and pretty soon they latched onto the idea that one of them should marry our doctor.'

'And of course he was so bored that he fell for it,' Sheila told her. This was a story told in tandem. The fact that there seemed to be some urgency about it was strange, but that was the way Rachel was hearing it. Maybe it was the way she was meant to be hearing it. 'He was feeling trapped by the needs of this community—by the needs of his grand-father. Beth was gorgeous and reminded him of a life he'd left behind. And after his parents' example I don't think he knew what a decent marriage was. So he married her. And had Toby.'

'Damned stupid…' Don shook his head. He looked side-ways at Rachel as if figuring out how much to tell—and then obviously decided that, unprofessional or not, he was going to tell anyway. 'It was never going to work. Beth married Hugo for all the wrong reasons and personally I don't think Hugo knew the right reasons to marry, either. Neither of them really knew what marriage was. Beth filled that house with all that weird stuff. She spent a fortune but still it didn't make her happy. She left him twice. Then, when she found she was pregnant, she walked out for ever. She wanted an abortion but he hated the idea. She compro-mised by leaving him. No, I know it doesn't make sense but, then, Beth didn't make sense to herself. She wasn't living with Hugo when Toby was born. She was living with some painter up in Sydney.'

'But still bleeding him dry,' Sheila added.

'And then she died.' Don looked sick at the memory. 'She had eclampsia. Apparently she and the guy she was living with were drinking too much. She didn't care about the baby—but it wasn't Toby who ended up suffering. She ig-nored the symptoms until she was far gone. Toby was born by Caesarean section but it was too late and that left our Hugo feeling dreadful. Guilt. He hadn't tried to make her come home. And Christine made the guilt worse.'

'Christine,' Rachel whispered.

'Of course, Christine.' Don shrugged. 'She stays on in this town because that's where she owns a house but she hates the place. Her paintings don't sell. She spends any money she gets on stupid things. You'd feel sorry for her if she wasn't so damned…superior. She's got no money of her own. She lives here and she won't let anyone forget Beth. She makes Hugo's guilt worse. "My Beth", she keeps saying as she shoves that shrine of a house down their throats. "We must never forget Toby's mother." The fact that they fought like cat and dog when Beth was alive…'

'She wants to marry Hugo.' Sheila was totally absorbed in her tale. Her ulcers were almost completely bandaged now but the old lady had a captive audience until they were finished and she wasn't letting go. 'And little by little she's wearing him down. Hugo has to let Toby spend time with Christine. It's the only contact the kid has with his mother's family. And she guilts him into keeping that house just as it was….'

Enough, Rachel thought, beginning to feel just a little desperate. The bandages were in place. This was entirely improper—doctor gossiping about another doctor with that doctor's patients and a nurse. Rachel rose to her feet and tried to look determined.

'I'm sure I need to see someone else.'

'No matter who you see they'll tell you the same thing,' Sheila retorted. 'Our Dr McInnes is being railroaded into marriage with another like the first. And she's not even a decent artist. What she does is horrible.'

Rachel was left wondering what was horrible. The thought of such a marriage—or Christine's artwork?

Maybe she knew.

'How did it go?'

Hugo collected her half an hour after he'd said he would. He'd been delayed by a minor crisis, he told her, but the look on his face told Rachel it hadn't been minor. He looked strained past endurance.

'What's wrong?' she asked, but he shook his head. Whatever it was, he didn't intend to share it.

'How did you manage at the nursing home?' he asked, changing the subject with more bluntness than tact.

She hesitated but his face was shuttered. This was a man accustomed to working on his own, she thought. He carried the responsibility for this town's health on his shoulders alone.

She could share but only as much as he wished her to share, and maybe it wasn't fair to push when she was here for such a short time.

So she concentrated on now. On the present.

'I love your oldies,' she told him. 'I now know not only their medical histories but also the history of everyone in Cowral.'

He managed a smile at that. 'Including mine?'

'Of course, including yours.' She settled into the passenger seat of his comfortable old family sedan and smiled across at him. She wanted him to smile. She wanted to take that look of strain away from around his eyes. 'How can you doubt it?'

'So...' He grimaced. 'Have they worked out your love life yet?'

'Mine?' She raised her eyebrows at that. 'I don't have a love life.'

'You have a husband.'

'That's right,' she said, and somehow kept her voice steady as he looked across at her.

'A husband. A love life. They're not the same thing?'

Were they? Once they were. A long time ago...

'Where are we going now?' she asked. He wasn't the only one who could change the subject. It was high time to move on from what was suddenly dangerous ground.

'I'll drop you at home for lunch and a rest while I—'

'While you keep working.'

'That's the plan.'

She shook her head. 'Nope. As plans go, it sucks.'

'Sorry?'

'I slept this morning while you worked. I've done a whole three hours' work while you, I suspect, have done about six. So why is it that now I get to be bored while you play doctor?'

He thought about it. 'You don't have to be bored. You could take Penelope for a walk.'

'I walked my feet off last night. I don't intend to walk anywhere for six months.'

'Then what do you want to do?'

'Have lunch now and then do something useful,' she said promptly. 'If I'm trapped in your house for the whole afternoon I might be forced to do something dire—like strip the brocade wallpaper from the living room.'

It had been the wrong thing to say. His face sort of set.

'Whoops,' Rachel said, not sounding in the least contrite. 'Don't tell me you like brocade.'

'I'm very grateful to Christine,' he said stiffly, which was a strange answer to a question that had hardly been asked.

'I'm grateful to Christine, too,' she told him, refusing to be dismayed into a guilty conscience 'But I'm not wearing brocade because of it. Or even the clothes she chose.'

'You'll hurt her feelings.'

'Really?' She looked at him in disbelief. 'Is that why you stick with the brocade? You really think that she'd be devastated if you said, "Thank you, Christine, you're very thoughtful but I don't like red and gold brocade. I like yellow."'

He frowned. 'What are you talking about? I don't like yellow.'

'Toby says you like yellow.'

'I don't.'

'You don't like Mr Addington's yellow car?'

The corners of his mouth twitched. The look of strain eased a bit and Rachel found herself smiling inside. Good. 'Who told you about Mr Addington's car?' he demanded.

'Toby. You do like it?'

'Of course I like it. It's a Ferrari.'

'Is that all you like about it? You'd like it better in red and gold?' She cocked her head to one side. 'Michael's Aston Martin is red. I hate that car.'

He raised his brows at that. Seemingly intrigued. 'So what is it with you and Michael? You hate his dog. You hate his car. You fight with the man in public and he abandons you in a town with a bushfire threatening.'

How did she answer that? She couldn't. She managed a shrug. 'So?'

The coldness of her tone didn't deflect him. He was still being nosy. 'I don't see that you have much of a marriage, Dr Harper.'

Should she tell him? No, she decided. His reaction to such a story was a complication she could do without. She hated telling people. She hated the way their faces shuttered down with shock and disbelief.

It was so much better to use Michael as a scapegoat. A pseudo-husband to hide the reality of pain. It was none of Hugo's business after all.

'I don't hate Penelope,' she told him, concentrating on the least of her issues with Michael. 'Whatever gave you that idea?'

'You don't love her!'

'She's sort of…goofy.' She grinned, moving right on. Steering fast from very dangerous personal relationships. 'Come on, Dr McInnes. Share your work with me. Don't sentence me to an afternoon with my goofy dog and your brocade walls.'

'I was planning to go out to the fire front,' Hugo told her. 'There's a command post out there. The teams are starting to show effects of smoke inhalation, heat exhaustion, burns. And the adrenaline isn't letting them stop.'

'Can I come with you?'

Those mobile eyebrows rose right up again. 'In those clothes?'

She looked down at herself. 'Maybe not,' she agreed cautiously. 'Maybe Mrs Sanderson could find me something a wee bit more suitable.'

'Maybe we'll grab a sandwich and then drop by the fire station,' he told her, the smile she was beginning to know and to love resurfacing from behind his eyes. 'I don't think even Mrs Sanderson does a couturier line in yellow fire-fighting apparel.'

The fire front was closer than they had expected.

Cowral Bay was on a spit about five miles from The Narrows, the mile-wide strip of land connecting Cowral to the mainland.

The Narrows were covered in mountainous bushland and all of it was burning. Hugo had expected to drive through to the far side of the first ridge, but there were roadblocks just as the land started to rise, and he was waved to a command post that had been brought further south.

'Hell.' Hugo pulled off the road and they stared together up at the ridge. The wind had died a little, which meant the billowing smoke was spiralling skyward and they could see flames bursting up over the mountains.

And for the first time, Rachel got nervous.

Up until now the fire had been a sort of backdrop to her real worries. It was the reason she was stuck here and noth-

ing else. Australians were accustomed to bushfires and this
was a bushfire. In bush.

But maybe it could turn to something worse?

She stared down at herself. The officer manning the fire
station had equipped her with heavy-duty overalls and big
leather boots, and she carried a hard hat. She'd looked at
herself in the mirror and had hooted with laughter. But
now…now she wasn't laughing.

'This is big,' she whispered, and Hugo looked over at her
and nodded.

'We lost a firefighter this morning.'

'You lost…'

'The wind changed,' he told her. 'He was trying to back-
burn and he'd gone too far from his team. He was cut off
and there was nothing anyone could do to save him. They
brought his body down just before I came to find you.'

She swallowed. No wonder he'd looked strained.

'Why didn't you tell me?'

'I just did.'

There'd been no need, Rachel thought. Or there had been
a need—a desperate need—but Hugo had been on his own
for too long to realise it. Sharing trauma, talking about it,
was the only way to cope in emergency medicine. But Hugo
coped alone. Somehow.

'What can I do?' she asked in a small voice, and he
looked across at her, assessing.

'If you really want to help…'

'I said I did, didn't I?' she snapped, suddenly angry. 'I'm
a member of your medical team, Dr McInnes. A team.
You're not on your own. Get used to it.'

'I didn't mean…'

'Just use me,' she said wearily. 'Use me.'

He cast her another strange look. But the situation was
dire. It was true. He did need her.

'The team who were with Barry when he died…they're still out there. They're due to come in at two. I'd like to see them all. There'll be real trauma. None of them would come off duty until their shift changed but I said I'd be available.'

'And you want teams to be briefed?'

'Last year in bushfire season I had a volunteer go home after suffering smoke inhalation. He didn't tell anyone he was having trouble breathing, then started coughing uncontrollably. By the time I saw him it was almost too late. I want the dangers spelled out to everyone, whether they've heard it five times or not. I want them to know to keep fluids on board. The professionals—even the well-trained volunteers—have been augmented now by helpers who mean well but haven't got two clues as to personal safety. They're working in teams but they get good ideas and go off by themselves. The guy this morning… He's in his sixties and he runs—ran—the local hardware store. He thought he knew it all. The fire chief has taken it hard. He's taken the volunteers through the safety drill but I want the medical bits spelled out in words of one syllable. I don't want any more deaths.'

'I can do that.'

'Make it sound dire,' Hugo told her. 'There's no second chances out there.'

'I can do dire.' She nodded. There was no laughter between them now. There was only medical need.

Which was how, half an hour later, overalled and booted and wearing her hard hat for heaven's sake— 'We wear them all the time when we're on duty,' she'd been told. 'It's a habit that makes sense not to break.' —Rachel found herself lecturing to a group of people who looked as out of place as she was.

Hugo was with the team of firefighters who'd lost their friend. She was with everyone else. Trying to sound knowledgeable. And authoritative.

She did. It was amazing what you could do when needs must.

'You stay hydrated,' she ordered. 'You carry water all the time. You never remove your hard hat. Ever. You keep your protective clothing on no matter how hot you get. You feel unwell for any reason, you get back here. For *any* reason. You start to cough, I want you back at base. You get any chest pain, a sore throat, your legs start aching—anything at all—you get back here fast. There's no medals for heroics. If you put your life at risk you'll put your whole team at risk. Now, before you go I want you to run past me individually and tell me a really brief medical history, and if there's anything at all you're vaguely worried about, you tell me now. You hear? Now!'

'She's amazing,' one of the firefighters told Hugo.

Miriam was one of the semi-trained volunteers. She'd been on the front line with Barry and she was suffering a nasty burn on her hand as well as shock from that morning's trauma. Hugo had what he needed to treat her on the spot but, having cleaned and dressed her burn, he was sending the woman home. Now they stood together in the clearing, watching Rachel assessing her firefighters thirty feet away. Each catching their breath before they moved on.

'She is amazing,' Hugo agreed. They could hear her voice, raised in authority. 'Bossy!'

'You'd think she'd been trained to do it.'

'Be bossy?' Hugo smiled. 'Maybe she has.'

'I wish I'd been a bit bossy,' Miriam said, and there was a load of bitterness and regret in her voice. 'Barry knew what we were told to do. We were just mopping up after backburning. If anything gets away, call for help, we were told, but when it flared he started fighting like a madman. The rest of us were retreating and he took it as a personal challenge. Then it was all around him. If I'd been a bit bossier…'

'Barry wouldn't have taken it from you,' Hugo said gently. Miriam was usually a clerk in the shire offices. She was so out of place here it was almost ridiculous. 'He'd never take orders from someone without authority.'

'He'd have taken orders from your Rachel,' Miriam told him. 'You just have to hear her. She seems…in charge.'

She did.

But what had Miriam said? 'Your Rachel…'

His Rachel. The words were unnerving. Miriam had meant them to denote that he and Rachel were a team but, looking across and seeing Rachel, it seemed almost more than that. She was listening to an elderly man who was telling her exactly why he should be allowed to fight the fires. Sam Nieve. Hell. It was obvious to anyone the man couldn't firefight. Hugo half rose to intervene but he didn't need to. He couldn't hear what she was telling him, but the man's shoulders didn't sag. Instead, his chest puffed out, he removed his helmet and he departed with an air of increased importance. His little car took off in the direction of the town and Hugo gave a sigh of relief.

Sam had a heart condition. He was the last person they'd want on the fire line but he was almost as stubborn as Barry. How had she convinced him?

If anyone could, Rachel could, he thought. The lady was amazing.

His Rachel?

No. The lady was married. The lady was…taken.

They worked solidly for three hours, but then it was time to return to the town. Hugo had patients in hospital and he had a clinic to run. He needed to return. The teams had changed over, the off-duty firefighters had gone back to the town to sleep and the on-duty members were lined up against the fire front.

The doctors would be needed again at change-over—or earlier if emergencies arose—but maybe because of the work they'd done, there'd be less chance of an emergency.

They could only hope.

'You did really well,' he told Rachel as they drove homeward, and she flushed.

'If we're forming an admiration society, can we make it mutual?'

'Nope. What did you tell Sam to make him give up his plans to fight fires?'

'You really want to know?'

'Yeah.'

'I used you.'

He raised his brows and grinned. 'You used me?'

'I told him you'd lost two patients in two days and there wasn't room in the funeral parlour for a third. I also told him if you lost someone else you'd be in for a breakdown and it'd be on his head if the town lost its doctor.'

'Gee, thanks very much,' he said faintly, but she hadn't finished yet.

'I told him brute strength wasn't all that was needed here. I told him that if the fire worsened, it was really important that everyone's roof is clear and they have their hoses ready. There are lots of people who are just blind when it comes to this type of thing.' She grinned, ignoring the fact that his brows had hit his hairline. 'I suspect, in fact, that Mr Nieve's own personal gutters around his roof are not as clean as they should be. I seemed to hit a nerve. Anyway, I suggested he contact the local school and borrow a few of the older kids and do a house-to-house check.'

Hugo whistled, seemingly totally astonished. 'Well done, you.'

'It's true,' she said gently.

'What's true?'

'You really don't want any more deaths.'

'What do you think?'

She looked at him, considering. 'I'm all for them,' she said at last, teasing for a smile. 'More deaths mean fewer patients and patients mess up your consulting rooms faster than anything I know.'

He laughed with her, but there wasn't a true smile behind his eyes.

'The two deaths...' she probed gently, and waited. He needed to talk, she suspected. There wouldn't be a lot of professional support in this one-doctor town.

And it seemed like it was professional support he was uncomfortable with.

She didn't let him off the hook. She waited and finally he shrugged and started to speak.

'Last night's death was expected,' he told her. 'It was Annie's time, but I was fond of her for all that.' He gave a twisted smile. 'Annie started making me chocolate cakes when Beth died and we've had a weekly chocolate cake ever since. And Barry...Barry was a pompous little prig who didn't deserve what happened to him. He has a sweet little wife and a couple of obnoxious kids who'll miss him for ever.'

Silence.

More silence.

'It's hard, this country practice,' Rachel said at last. She was combing pieces of debris from her hair with her fingers. She'd taken her hard hat off before she'd got back in the car, which had been a mistake. The air was thick with falling ash, and most of it seemed to have ended up in her hair. 'You get attached.'

'Something you don't do?'

'It's not all that easy getting attached when you work in emergency medicine,' she agreed. 'I keep track of some patients but not many.'

'So when you finish up a shift, the day's over.'

'Pretty much.'

'It'd be a great life,' Hugo said softly, and Rachel didn't miss the note of bitterness in his voice.

'What, so you'd really like to swap?'

'I'd just like to turn off sometimes,' he told her. 'This town... I came here for a few years to look after my ailing grandfather and I've never been able to leave.'

'Because you can't get anyone else to replace you?'

'Partly.'

'And partly what else?' She'd twisted sideways to watch him. They were nearly back in town now—their time for intimacy was almost over and she regretted it. She liked this big, gentle man with the laughing eyes. She liked him a lot. It seemed such a shame that he was meant for...the likes of Christine?

She'd seen the way Christine had looked at Hugo. Hugo may have married one sister but by the look in Christine's eyes and by the accounts of local gossip he was destined to marry the other.

But Hugo wasn't talking about Christine. Or he was, but only in that she was part of the tapestry of Toby's life. 'Partly because my life is here,' he told her. 'Toby's life. The people here love him. He has Myra and Christine and...so many people. He has the freedom of the place—there's not a soul in Cowral Bay who doesn't know who he is and watches out for him.'

'And in return you watch out for them,' she said softly.

He was concentrating on turning into the hospital car park but it wasn't the concentration that was causing the set look around his mouth. He cared. He'd certified the deaths of two of Cowral's own in the past twenty-four hours and it had bitten deep.

Rachel saw deaths most days. She worked in a big city emergency department.

Two deaths wouldn't affect her like this.

Maybe they should. Maybe she should be more involved.

She was involved enough. How could she be any more involved than she was right now?

She should be home...

'It must be amazing,' Hugo said, 'to leave work at night and be free to go to the movies, go out to a restaurant—do anything you want.'

He had to be kidding. If he knew how much she hated eating out... And when had she last gone to a movie? Going to movies on her own sucked. 'I have responsibilities,' she said stiffly, and he nodded.

'Of course you do. Penelope. Michael.'

'Michael's not—'

'You're right. Michael's none of my business.' He cut her off as he switched off the engine. 'But I'm interested. What do you do with the rest of your life? How do city doctors without kids operate? It's a world away from what I know.'

'You did it once.'

'It's so long ago I've forgotten. I wouldn't mind remembering.'

Remembering what? He was talking about the giddy social life Michael enjoyed, Rachel knew, and that was so far away from her own experience that it was ridiculous. She closed her eyes. What was the point in explaining? There wasn't one. This man had enough on his shoulders without burdening him with her personal tragedy.

'You wouldn't be interested,' she said flatly. 'And you have work to do. Is there anything else I can do to help?'

He looked at her and once again she had the feeling he saw more than she wanted him to. But he couldn't know. How could he possibly know about Craig?

He didn't. Of course he didn't. He was shaking his head, moving on.

'You've done enough.'

'You're doing clinic?'

'For a couple of hours.'

'So Toby and I will see you at dinner.'

'That's right. So you can take your overalls off, Dr Harper, and turn into a guest again. Exercise your dog or something.'

'Right.'

'I'll see you later.'

End of conversation. But he was still watching her. His eyes still held hers.

He should turn away, she thought. He should get out of the car.

He didn't. They were somehow…locked?

It was a strange sensation. Stupid. Senseless. He had things to do. She was a married woman and they had no link.

They did have a link. They were just looking at each other. Seeing…

Seeing past the façade. Seeing what was really behind it.

She stared into his face and she could see the battering this man had suffered over the years. The loneliness. The wanting.

How could she see that? She didn't know. But see it she

did, and if she could read so much in his face, how much more could he read in hers?

This was ridiculous. She had things to do. Dogs to walk. Hours to fill before she saw him again.

Ridiculous!

Somehow Rachel managed to break the moment—break the link. She climbed from the car and slammed the door with more force than was needed. The slam was a statement.

'I'm going to take a shower,' she told him, and if her voice wasn't quite steady there wasn't a darned thing she could do about it. 'I'll see you later.'

She walked away, leaving Hugo staring after her.

CHAPTER SIX

HE DIDN'T have a clue what was going on.

Hugo worked his way through half a dozen patients and maybe it was just as well there was nothing serious, because his attention was definitely elsewhere. Or maybe it'd be better if there was something serious, he decided. Maybe his thoughts needed to be hauled right back to work. Not on some slip of a doctor whose eyes made him smile. Whose smile made him chuckle...

Whose smile made him twist inside.

How long had it been since someone had made him feel like this? Some woman?

Never, he thought as he carefully wound wet bandage around Tom Harris's arm. Tom had fallen and broken his forearm while clearing undergrowth around his house when the fires had started four days ago. Hugo had put the initial plaster on loosely because of inflammation but the arm had settled now and it could be fixed more securely into its casing.

Tom, though, was a man of few words. He didn't want to chat, so Hugo's attention stayed right where it was. On Rachel.

Why was it on Rachel?

She was married, he told himself. Happily married for all he knew. Sure, the man she'd been with at the dog show had seemed a creep, but the nicest of women found partners in the strangest of places. She hadn't said a word about her marriage being unhappy.

Maybe she couldn't. Maybe the man was violent.

No.

He thought back to his medical training, to the one question he'd been told could predict violence in marriages in almost every case. He'd used it time and again with sometimes astonishing results.

'Is there any time in the last couple of years where you've felt afraid of your husband?'

He thought of Rachel and he knew instinctively that she'd shake her head if he directed his question at her. She'd been angry at Michael at the dog show but she hadn't been afraid of him. She'd flung those car keys at him with such force that the memory still made him smile.

'You thinking of the new lady doctor?' Tom asked, and Hugo nearly dropped his bandages.

'No. I was thinking how good this arm is looking.'

'People don't smile like that thinking about a sixty-year-old fisherman's broken arm,' Tom said dourly, though there was the hint of laughter in his eyes.

'Why not? You have a very nice arm,' Hugo tossed back, and Tom's face creased into reluctant laughter.

'Yeah, and yours is sexy and all as well,' he retorted. 'But I bet our Rachel has a sexier one.'

Our Rachel... How quickly had the community taken her as one of its own?

'The lady's married,' Hugo snapped before he could stop himself, and Tom's grin broadened.

'So I'm on the right track, then.'

'Look—'

'It's nothing to do with me, mate,' Tom told him. 'I'm just here to get an arm fixed. You're the one who has to go home tonight and sleep in the same house. Married or not.'

Hugo shook his head, thoroughly confused. 'I can't...'

'Yeah, you can,' Tom said encouragingly, knowing exactly what he was thinking. Like it or not. 'Or you can at least try.'

It was well past dinnertime when a weary Hugo arrived home. What a day, and there was still a ward round to do before he could sleep. Even so, he was aware of a lifting of his spirits as he walked from the hospital across the lawn to the house. It'd be different tonight. Rachel would be there.

She certainly was. He walked in the back door and instead of a formally set table, with Myra waiting to serve up chops and three vegetables—her standard fare, to be expected at least three times a week—he walked in to find Rachel packing an enormous picnic basket. Toby was sitting on the table, poking things into its depths, and his small face was lit up with excitement.

'We're going to the beach for tea,' he told his father before Hugo could open his mouth. 'Or for your tea and an after-tea picnic for us. Rachel says it's so hot and stuffy that if she doesn't get a swim she'll expire.'

'She will, too.' Rachel was back in those extraordinary yellow clothes again. Her wonderful clothes. 'And the dogs are going stir-crazy.' She gestured to the two dogs, who were lying on the floor eyeing the picnic basket with a devotion that said they'd already tested the contents. 'Have you finished for the day, Dr McInnes?'

'I need to do a ward round before—'

'I've done your ward round,' she told him before he could finish. 'Elly talked me through every patient in the hospital and there's no need for you to see any of them again tonight.' She corrected herself. 'You might like to look in on Kim to check that her obs are still OK before you go to bed, but as of twenty minutes ago they were fine. There's no change in the fire crews for another two hours, and things seem relatively settled. The wind's forecast to strengthen tomorrow, which means havoc might break loose, so Toby and I figured we might have some fun while the going's good. That's now.'

'The nursing home—'

'Yep. There are a couple of oldies who need checks. Mrs Bosworth's breathing is cause for concern. I've told Don we'll stop in on the way.'

'The way...'

'To the beach.'

She tossed a bag of grapes into the picnic basket and beamed at him, expectant. So did Toby. The dogs looked up and wagged a tail apiece and he could swear they were beaming, too.

'I can't,' he said faintly, and Rachel's beam slipped immediately. He found himself staring at a lady with her arms crossed, schoolmarm-like, and a martial glint in her eye.

'Why ever not?'

'If I'm needed—'

'You're needed at the nursing home and Toby and I have agreed we'll watch television in the oldies' sitting room while you do the doctor bit. Or vice versa, but Mrs Bosworth's anxious and she's asking for you.' She smiled. 'You must have something in your bedside manner that I don't.' Her smile faded. 'Or Hazel Bosworth knows you and it's a familiar face she needs when she's frightened. But after that... The smoke's not so bad that it'll be awful. We have cold sausages. We have cold drinks and fresh bread and some of Toby's wonderful lamingtons. Your bathing costume's already packed and we're already wearing ours under our clothes, so what other objections would you care to make?'

Hugo couldn't think of any. He couldn't think of any at all. How long since he'd had a picnic on the beach?

'Please? Can we go, Daddy? Can we go?' Toby was jiggling with excitement. Under the table Penelope and Digger were jiggling as well.

'Yes,' he said promptly, before he changed his mind and got sensible. 'Yes, we can.'

Why not?

The nursing home was quieter than they'd expected. 'Most of the residents have seen scores of bushfires in their time,' Don told them. 'They're not panicking.' He gave a rueful smile. 'Most of them gave up their households of precious possessions when they came in here. It makes a difference when there's not so much to lose. Even Mrs Bosworth... Her breathing's dreadful, Hugo. She has emphysema and we can't get the smoke out of the atmosphere. She's so sick. But when I told her I was going to call you she said not to bother—that the doctors would have more than enough to cope with tonight, and if she died then it was her time. Age puts a different perspective on things.'

Not just age.

It was experience, Rachel thought as Hugo disappeared to see to Mrs Bosworth's breathing problems and she settled to wait with Toby. Once upon a time in another life she'd collected porcelain. She remembered Craig coming home from football, bouncing in the front door full of his triumph, shouting to her. Whizzing her round in triumph, crashing one of her porcelain statuettes off the hall table.

She'd been angry.

Dear God, she'd been angry.

The porcelain was long sold. It had been many years since Rachel had seen anything more important than people. Life.

Now.

This minute.

Mrs Bosworth was settling. Hugo was emerging, discussing her condition with Don. The oxygen rate was up to maximum now and he'd given her a relaxant. Fear was making her breathing faster, causing more problems.

Because, of course, there was fear. Possessions could be abandoned. But not so life.

Sometimes life was wonderful.

Life was now, Rachel thought with quiet satisfaction as they reached the shoreline. Tomorrow might well be ghastly, but for now…for now there was this moment.

The locals had too much sense to be sitting on a smoky stretch of beach. Everyone not directly committed to the fire effort was supporting those who were. Tired people chose to stay indoors.

But now was too good to waste.

The tension eased from Hugo's tired mind almost as soon as his toes touched the sand.

The wind had miraculously dropped to almost nothing. The fine haze of eucalypt-filled smoke was even soothing. If there hadn't been the possibility that it might threaten the town when the wind came up, he could almost enjoy it.

Or maybe he could enjoy it anyway. How long since he'd hauled off his shoes and spent the evening on the beach?

He wouldn't have thought to do it.

Rachel had thought of it. Rachel…

'Maybe we won't light fires to warm our sausages,' Rachel was suggesting, as the dogs went careering like mad things along the shore, and Hugo could only agree.

'Wise idea. One spark and we'd have every hose in town pointed straight at us. There are people on the lookout right now. Sparks drift for miles and are a threat all by themselves.'

'The town won't burn, will it, Daddy?' Toby asked, and

Hugo hauled himself together. He'd been sounding too solemn.

Maybe he'd been sounding too solemn for far, far too long.

'No. The town won't burn. There's no wind at all tonight so the backburners can really get things under control.' He took a deep breath. For now—for this small fragment of time—he could forget about fires. He could even—amazingly—forget about medicine. He could concentrate on what was important. 'Let's eat,' he suggested, and he could feel the tension easing out of him still more.

Rachel was smiling again, as if she knew that some invisible barrier had been broached. But it seemed she wasn't pushing.

'I'm swimming first,' she told him. 'Toby and I snacked while we waited for you. You have a sausage or two and join us—but don't eat too much. It'd be a shame to have to wait your requisite half an hour because you were scared of cramps.'

'That's an old wives' tale,' he said, and she raised mocking eyebrows.

'It's the medicine my granny taught me. Are you saying my Granny's medicine—and therefore my medicine—is wrong?'

He thought about that. He thought about the way he was feeling. Free. Almost light-headed. There was an anticipation in his heart that had nothing to do with common sense and everything to do with the way this lady smiled. Dr Rachel Harper's medicine.

'No, but—'

'Good,' she told him, her smile showing him she was aware of the fact that he was confused and she intended enjoying it. 'Mind your sausages, Dr McInnes. Toby and I are going for a swim.'

*   *   *

So Hugo sat and ate and watched his small son and this strange city doctor cavort in the shallows.

Rachel was the strangest creature, he decided. She was part girl, part woman. Part professional doctor, part kid who was searching for fun and laughter.

There was so much about her he didn't understand.

The hardest thing of all was to reconcile her marriage to Michael. To a doctor who'd risked a girl's life...

Hugo was under no illusion that Michael couldn't have redirected the helicopter. He would have heard the impassioned plea to return. He'd have heard how desperately ill Kim was. Hugo himself had talked to the pilot and he'd heard the pilot turn and talk to Michael. It had been Michael the helicopter had come to collect: to have forced him to stay in the air would have been nothing short of abduction.

Michael therefore must have been complicit in the decision not to bring the helicopter back to take Kim to safety.

And Michael was married to Rachel.

Rachel, who was gorgeous.

'Hey, Toby, spin,' Rachel was calling. Waist deep in the shallows, she had Toby high in her arms and was spinning him like the sails of a small windmill. She spun and spun while the dogs barked and barked and Hugo couldn't stop himself from grinning in delight.

Enough. He'd eaten enough.

'One more sausage and I'll cramp,' he told himself, and strolled into the water to join them. At the water's edge he paused, laughing at the expression of joy on Toby's face as he whirled faster and faster. Hugo chuckled out loud—and then his chuckle died.

Rachel and Toby had shed their outer clothes at the water's edge. From where Hugo had sat thirty yards up the beach, Rachel had looked beautiful. In her crimson, one-piece bathing suit, cut to reveal every gorgeous curve, she'd been glowingly lovely.

But closer...

Closer there were scars.

He stared, caught by the incongruity of it. By the questions. The fine white lines were the marks of a skilled plastic surgeon. Hugo could see that. But no skill could entirely cover the trauma Rachel's body must have once endured.

When? A long time ago, he thought, looking at the way the scarring had faded—fine lines blending into her near-perfect skin.

She was laughing and whirling and she and Toby turned to face him, glowing with happiness.

He didn't get his face in order fast enough.

She stopped whirling and set Toby down on his feet. Carefully. 'What?' she said.

'You've been hurt.' He spoke without thinking and then could have kicked himself. He could have said nothing. He should have. He could have pretended he hadn't noticed.

A non-medical person might not have noticed.

No. She was so lovely that any man would look at Rachel long and hard. The fine lines of scarring didn't detract from her loveliness but they were unmistakable.

'Car accident,' she said shortly, answering his question before he'd voiced it. 'Eight years ago.'

A car accident. Of course. He gave himself another mental kick. Why had his thoughts gone straight to this Michael character he was starting so stupidly to dislike?

These weren't the type of scars that were the result of battering from an aggressive husband—and anyone could see that Rachel wasn't a battered wife. She was probably a hugely contented wife who occasionally threw car keys at her husband. Wives did that.

Beth had thrown more than car keys at him!

But what was he thinking of? He was still staring at Rachel as if he were stupid.

'I'm sorry,' he told her. 'I didn't mean to stare. It must have been some accident.'

'It was.' She looked as if she was about to say more and then closed her lips together, tight.

'Internal injuries? Fractures?'

'You name it, I had it.' She shrugged. 'It was a long time ago. Bodies heal. Mostly.'

There was a depth of bitterness in her words that he couldn't help but hear. Maybe someone had died in the accident? Someone she loved? But the blank look on her face was a shield all by itself. Keep off, the look said. Don't go there.

So he didn't. Even though he badly wanted to.

It was none of his business.

'It looks like you've had some great corrective surgery,' he managed, and her smile came flooding back. There was relief there and the beginnings of laughter.

'I have, haven't I?' For heaven's sake, was she laughing at his discomfort? 'There's a wonderful plastic surgeon in Sydney who calls me his masterpiece. I sometimes get the feeling he'd like to hang me on his wall for show and tell!'

Rachel was so damned courageous. He just had to look at that scarring to know the trauma that lay behind it. And that brief look of pain had told him there was even more…

'You are a masterpiece,' he said softly, and she flushed. She wasn't giving in to her discomposure, though. She moved right on to discomfit him further.

'You know, you're not too bad yourself.' She scooped Toby up into her arms and twinkled. 'What do you reckon, Toby? Don't you think your dad has the greatest six-pack you've ever seen?'

'Six-pack?' Toby was giggling, entranced.

And entranced was a good way to describe his father. Hugo was enchanted by this vivacious slip of a girl. She was soaking wet, her soft brown curls were lying in dripping tendrils around her face, her eyes were dancing…

'You know six-packs,' she told Toby, seemingly unaware of the riot she was causing in Hugo's solar plexus. Or somewhere. Some nerve centre he'd hardly been aware he possessed. 'Six-packs are cans of beer tied up together. You look at your daddy's chest and tell me if it doesn't look just like that?'

Good grief!

It was as much as Hugo could do not to blush. He swallowed, tried to think of something to say, couldn't, so did the only thing he could think of.

He dived straight under the water and left them alone.

He stayed out of their way for about a quarter of an hour. It's the equivalent of a cold shower, he told himself, and that was what he needed. He swam and he swam, using the rhythm of his strokes to try and settle his brain.

What was happening to him? Rachel was a married woman. She was a colleague who'd been trapped here by the fire. As soon as the wind changed and the fires burned back on themselves she'd be out of here. He had no business to think of her as he was thinking.

He had no choice. He was definitely thinking.

He swam.

It had to end some time. It had been a huge day and a man could only swim so far, regardless of what demons were driving him.

Toby and Rachel had taken themselves up the beach and were engaged in building the world's biggest sandcastle. As Hugo towelled himself dry and strolled up the beach to join them, Rachel shifted back to admire their handiwork. She glanced up at his face—which he was still trying to control—and she chuckled.

'Hey, don't get your knickers in a twist by a comment on a six-pack.' She grinned. 'It's what we women put up with all the time. That was the female equivalent of a wolf whistle.'

He stared. 'Sorry?'

Her smile widened as his discomfiture deepened. 'Sorry yourself. OK, I'm sorry about the six-pack remark but you did get personal first.'

'So I did,' he said faintly. 'So I guess I'm sorry, too.'

'Actually, I'm not sorry,' she said with a sideways, very thoughtful look. 'For the expression on your face—it was well worth it.'

Had it been worth it? He stared down at her and she smiled back, enigmatic and lovely and thoroughly confusing.

It couldn't last. He might be directionless but Rachel at least was focused. Toby was lifting a football from the bottom of the picnic basket and was kicking it across the sand without much hope.

'Given up on the sandcastle?' Rachel asked him.

'Yeah.' The little boy looked down at his plastic football and sighed. 'I brought this with me tonight 'cos Bradley Drummond says I can't drop-kick. I gotta learn how to drop-kick and Dad can't drop-kick for nuts.'

'You can't drop-kick?' Rachel stared at Hugo, amazed.

'I played basketball,' he said in explanation, and she looked at him as if it wasn't an explanation at all.

'I can't believe it. A man who plays basketball… What use is a six-pack in basketball?'

'Hey!'

'Say no more.' She wiped her hands on non-existent trousers, and wriggled her shoulders—a player prepared to launch into a tackle. 'A basketball player... Good grief. Toby, lad, give me the ball.'

'Can you drop-kick?' he asked shyly, and she nodded.

'I was taught by the best. My husband was the world's absolutely top drop-kicker. Or so he told me and who am I to doubt it? And he taught me.'

'Gee,' Toby, said, impressed.

'Gee is right. So there you go. Drop-kick lessons coming up. And you, Dr McInnes, stop worrying and have some dinner,' she told him. 'You've hardly eaten anything.' She flashed him a look that was almost a warning. 'Sausages and lamingtons and grapes. Eat. For heaven's sake, Hugo, let's keep life simple.'

Keep life simple? He didn't know what she was talking about.

Or maybe he did, but he sure as heck didn't want to admit it.

It had gone way past being simple but at least it was peaceful. Miraculously his cellphone stayed silent. It might be the calm before the storm but for these few hours there seemed no medical need, and no need at all for them to rush their picnic and head for home.

With their drop-kick lessons completed to their mutual satisfaction, Rachel and Toby turned their attention back to food. They polished off sausages with gusto.

'It's our second dinner,' Rachel declared, 'and it's much nicer the second time around.' They ate their fill of lamingtons and finished off with a Thermos of coffee, with lemonade for Toby, and then Toby snuggled down on beach towels beside them and drifted toward sleep. One six-year-old had had a truly excellent day.

'We don't do this often enough,' Hugo said ruefully, running his fingers through Toby's sand-and salt-stiff hair. But he wasn't totally focused on his son. He was still letting Rachel's words drift around his head. *My husband was the world's absolutely top drop-kicker.* He didn't like it.

He didn't want to think about Rachel's husband.

And it seemed Rachel's thoughts were travelling on a similar route.

'Christine doesn't like the beach?'

'Christine?' His gaze jerked to hers, startled. 'What's it got to do with Christine?'

'She is the lady you intend to marry,' Rachel said gently, and watched his face.

He said nothing.

Christine… That relationship had been on the backburner for so long that he hardly knew. When had it started? This assumption that he'd end up with his sister-in-law?

He didn't know when it had begun. She'd just been there. Even when Beth had been alive, Christine had done the organising, acting as go-between in their increasingly turbulent marriage, suggesting, steering…

Oh, there had been nothing untoward in their relationship during the marriage. There was nothing untoward in it now. It was just drifting…

Toward marriage? Maybe. And why? Because it was easier. Because the town was waiting.

Christine was waiting.

'It's been six years,' Rachel said softly. 'Isn't it about time you married the woman?'

'Who told you we were getting married?'

'Christine did,' Rachel told him. She glanced down at Toby who was sleeping now, deeply unconscious. 'Tonight. When I told her we were coming to the beach. I was told in no uncertain terms to keep myself to myself. I've never actually been given the scarlet woman treatment before, but I copped it tonight.'

For heaven's sake. Hugo's face set in anger. Of all the stupid… She had no right.

Did she have a right?

He hadn't given her reason to think otherwise, he admitted to himself. Lately, Christine had taken to kissing him goodbye, and a few weeks ago he'd let himself kiss her back. Not as he'd kissed her in the past, brother-in-law to sister-in-law, but more. Man to woman.

Hell, why?

He knew why. He'd needed to so much. Just to feel the touch of a woman in his arms.

But it had still felt wrong, even though Beth had been dead these six years. So he'd pulled back. Apologised. But Christine had smiled and he'd known that she was waiting.

And he hadn't said no. He hadn't said it could never work. In truth, he'd been wondering…

Six years was a long time and this was a tiny town. In this confined environment he couldn't look at a woman without that woman getting the wrong idea. Affairs were impossible. He was so damned lonely and he was hungry…

He wasn't hungry for Christine, he conceded to himself, looking at the woman in front of him and accepting what was becoming clearer by the minute. He was hungry for Rachel.

Rachel was unavailable. What had she said about her husband? *The world's absolutely top drop-kicker…* There was a wealth of affection in the way she'd said it that had been unmistakable.

Maybe Christine was all there was.

'So you are going to marry her?'

Rachel was watching him with the air of an inquisitive

sparrow. Furious, with himself as well as her, he started to haul the picnic things together.

'I think it's time we took Toby home.'

'Toby's asleep. He can't be any more asleep at home than he is right now. And you haven't answered the question.'

'It's none of your business.'

'Mmm, but I thought we'd agreed we'd already been impolite. We may as well keep going, don't you think?'

'No,' he said, goaded, and she smiled.

'You started it.'

He had, he conceded, with his talk of her scarring. But he had no intention of continuing.

Rachel had no intention of stopping.

'Toby doesn't like Christine much,' she told him. 'Neither does Myra. Do you think Christine would soften with the brocade-remembering-Beth thing if you married?'

'Look—'

'I wouldn't want to live with it.' She stretched her legs out full length, admiring her sandy toes. She had beautiful crimson toenails.

Very distracting toenails.

'I can see why you'd want to, of course!' she conceded. 'She's lovely. Is Christine very like your wife was?'

'Will you cut it out?' He was half laughing, half angry. 'Why don't we talk about you for a change?'

'Like what about me?' She was still admiring her toenails.

'Like what is it between you and your husband? You were fighting like cat and dog at the weekend. It can't be much of a marriage.'

The laughter left her face. She'd been teasing him—it had been light-hearted banter—but suddenly there was no banter left. There was a long silence. Then…

'No,' she said at last, and she spoke so softly he had to

strain to hear what she was saying. 'No, I don't have much of a marriage.'

He shouldn't go further. He should stop this potentially hurtful conversation right now.

He couldn't. The devil—or something—was driving him. He had to push.

'Yet you're criticising me for potentially making a love-less marriage?'

'Whoa…' Her eyes flashed at that. 'I didn't say a word about a loveless marriage,' she retorted, spirit re-entering her voice with a vengeance. 'I may not have much of a marriage but I surely went into it with love.'

'Yet you want out?'

The conversation had become suddenly so intense he could hardly breathe. Hell, how had this happened? He watched her face and her eyes were blind, as if she was consumed by panic.

'I'm out now, aren't I?' she whispered. 'Dear God, I shouldn't be, but I'm out.'

He didn't know what was happening. He didn't under-stand. All he knew was that he'd hurt her somehow, and hurt her badly. 'Rachel, don't look like that.'

'Look like what?'

'Like there's something inside you that's tearing apart.'

'I'm not… It's not…'

Her hands were fumbling, trying to collect the picnic things together, but he could see she wasn't thinking of what she was doing. Her hands weren't connected to her thoughts and her eyes were still so pain-filled that he found himself reaching out, grasping her fingers between his. Holding…

She didn't pull away.

She didn't move.

How long they stayed there he could never afterwards tell. The night was creeping in through the smoky haze. The sun had slipped unnoticed, behind the mountains, behind the distant fires. The beach was deserted.

All was still, apart from the soft hush, hush, hush of the waves slipping into shore, one after the other.

Endless.

Time was nothing. There was nothing. This had started as comfort—hadn't it?—but now it was more. Deeper. For this moment there was just this man and this woman and a meeting that neither could understand, that neither wanted, that simply was.

Still their hands held. It was their eyes doing the talking, searching, locked to each other and discovering in each a link. A bond. An aching need and a knowledge that in each other pain could be assuaged.

The moment stretched on.

He should break his hold. He should release her hands, pull back...

But still his eyes searched hers and with every moment that passed the need to do more became increasingly compulsive.

Inescapable.

One man. One woman. One moment.

He pulled her into his arms and he kissed her.

What was she doing here? Rachel hardly knew. All she knew was that the moment Hugo's fingers touched hers, her mind shut down to everything that wasn't him.

Toby was asleep. The dogs were far off, fruitlessly chasing gulls in endless circles around the beach. There were no witnesses to what was happening here.

There was no problem with witnesses. No one would gainsay her this pleasure. Dottie had told her that as she'd packed the gorgeous lingerie and pushed her out the door to what she'd thought would be a romantic weekend with Michael.

Only it would never have worked. Even if Michael had been…nice, she could never have let him near her. The guilt had still been with her. The overriding bitterness at what could have been.

But all of that was lost the moment Hugo's hands touched hers. He pulled her into him and as his mouth claimed hers and as she melted effortlessly into him, all she felt was joy.

Oh, the pleasure. The aching wonder. Eight years of sorrow and loneliness were all dispelled in this one kiss. In this meeting of bodies, one with the other.

It was a kiss, but it was so much more than a kiss. It was a melting of barriers, a moving forward, a reaffirmation of life itself.

She couldn't pull away. She knew she should but she hadn't the strength. Rachel, who'd been so strong for so long, was falling now as she hadn't let herself ever fall. She'd been alone and now…she was home. She was where she belonged. Hugo was kissing her and she was moving from an old life into a new, like a butterfly emerging from a faded and torn chrysalis to begin a new life.

Hugo.

Life or death. Living or dying.

I choose…life.

The dogs disturbed them. The flock of gulls they'd been chasing finally wheeled out to sea. Delirious with excitement, the dogs came hurtling up the beach, soaking wet. They landed on the picnic rug and proceeded to shake what seemed gallons of seawater over everyone.

Including Toby. He woke and whimpered a little. Hugo pulled away for an instant and it was enough. To let reality in.

To let Rachel's reality sink in.

What was she doing?

And there they all were—the old doubts, the fears and the loneliness and the endless future. They hadn't disappeared. They'd been subsumed by the moment but they were still there.

The pressure of Hugo's mouth was still on her lips. She put her fingers up to touch them but Hugo was before her. Toby had stirred and settled, the dogs had wheeled away again and he was catching her fingers in his lovely big hands, and there was such a look of tenderness on his face that she must surely melt...

'Rachel...'

'No,' she faltered, and pulled away. Reluctantly, he released her. He watched her, his eyes calm. Something had changed for him, too, she thought frantically. He *knew*.

He couldn't know. He mustn't.

'Rachel, what's wrong?'

'I'm married,' she said, and there was such a blunt finality about the words that the look of tenderness shuttered down on his face as if it had never been.

'You said...you wanted out.'

'I didn't.' She was hauling herself together now—somehow. She had to get off this beach. She had to get away from this man.

She had to leave.

'I don't want—' he started, but she was before him.

'Neither do I.' She was close to tears. Here she was, lying again. She wanted Hugo so much that she was tearing apart and she could feel herself disintegrating. 'I-it's almost dark,' she stammered. 'You have to check Kim. I...I'm tired. I need my bed. Please, Hugo, can we go?'

She rose and hauled her beach towel around herself like

a shield. It was stupid. Nothing could protect her from what she was feeling. Nothing.

'Can we go?' she whispered again. 'Please, Hugo. I don't need this. I can't… I can't.'

And there was nothing for them to do but to leave.

There was nothing for Hugo to do but to look at her with hungry eyes and a hopeless heart.

Kim was fine when he arrived back at the hospital, but Hugo took his time with the injured teenager. He hardly knew why. Kim was deeply asleep. Her exhausted parents had finally decided to cease their vigil and leave their daughter in the nurses' care. Hugo could have simply glanced at the observation chart and left, but instead he carefully checked the wound, unwinding the bandages and surveying his hand-iwork with care. David, the ginger-haired nurse who was in charge tonight, watched with thoughtful appreciation.

'You know she's fine. I checked the leg myself a couple of hours ago. No temp, the leg's as pink as the other one, she's having pain but it seems to be settling—even her parents are relaxing now. Why not you, Dr McInnes?'

'I'm relaxing,' Hugo snapped, and David grinned.

'Yeah, and I'm a monkey's uncle. You're tense as all get-out. You're not expecting any dramas here, are you?'

Hugo looked down at Kim's face. The fifteen-year-old was sleeping soundly, exhausted from the effects of trauma and relaxing deeply into the drugs he was using for pain-killing. She looked…fine. No, he wasn't expecting any trauma here. Thanks to Rachel.

What was Rachel's story?

Why did he need to know?

'She'll be OK,' he managed, but David was still watching him.

'You're avoiding going home?' David asked softly, and Hugo winced. Was he so transparent?

'No.'

But David didn't believe him. He was a fine nurse and part of that was that he read people well. 'There's nothing here for you to do,' he told Hugo, his eyes still thoughtful. 'The last of the fire crews rang in half an hour ago. Because there's no wind up on the ridge, there's been no dramas at all—not even a bad case of smoke in the eyes. You can go home to bed, Dr McInnes.'

'Yeah.'

'And you ought to.' David was watching him with an intensity that Hugo found unnerving. 'The forecast for to-morrow is horrible. If they don't hold the firebreaks...'

'The town will be safe. The river...'

'The river will hold it this side. But the other side...'

'You know the plan is for everyone to get over here and stay.' Hugo shifted uneasily, thinking it through. Forcing his mind away from Rachel and onto the urgency of what lay ahead. 'People's homes are insured. They've had warning to leave. They'll come.'

'People do damned stupid things. Get yourself to bed, Hugo.' David's voice was suddenly rough with concern. 'You know you're going to be needed.'

'I'll be fine.'

Silence. Then... 'At least you have Dr Harper.' David's eyes were still probing. 'Rachel,' he amended, and watched Hugo's face twist. David looked even more thoughtful. Hmm, the expression on his face said. Was that the way the wind blew, then?

It wasn't up to Hugo to enlighten him. 'Yeah, at least I have Rachel,' he snapped, and shoved his hands deep into his pockets and glared.

'So go to bed and thank your stars you have her while you do,' David told him.

'Right.' He was right. Of course he was right. Go to bed and be thankful...

To bed. To sleep? That was a joke!

And Rachel?

She lay awake and thought about Craig.

But she didn't ring Dottie.

CHAPTER SEVEN

RACHEL was awake before he was. As Hugo appeared in the kitchen for breakfast just after six, Rachel burst through the screen door, a dog attached to a leash in either hand.

She stopped short when she saw him. Discomfited. The dogs bounded across the kitchen to greet him and he bent to hug them. Giving himself time to collect himself.

The dogs were great. Afghan and mongrel were becoming fast friends.

Michael would have kittens. Aristocracy mixing with the hoi-polloi. Ouch.

Michael. There he was, thinking about Michael again. Why the hell couldn't he keep himself from thinking about Michael?

Rachel was wearing short shorts, and a crop top and sandals. She was all bare legs and glowing face and shiny hair.

How could he not think of Michael?

He had to get himself together.

'Hi,' he tried, and waited.

'Hi.'

'You've been to the beach.' That much was obvious. The dogs were damp and sand-coated, and Penelope the Afghan had such a look of bliss on her dopey face he almost felt sorry for her that she had to return to the city. To Michael.

There he was again.

Rachel had to return to the city to Michael. The thought was enough to make the beginnings of his smile fade completely.

'I couldn't sleep,' Rachel told him, and the tension es-

calated by about a mile. She hadn't been able to sleep.
Neither had he. Because…

What was he thinking of? Heck, he had better…more
serious things to think about than why Rachel hadn't been
able to sleep.

Like a bushfire.

'It's bad,' Rachel told him, moving on before he could.
'The wind came up before the sun did. The dogs and I could
see the flames rising higher on the ridge while we waited
for the sunrise.'

How long had she been on the beach? It didn't matter. It
couldn't matter. Move on…

'Crisis today,' he said, and turned his back to put on the
kettle. He was wearing his boxer shorts and nothing else.
That was what he always wore while he ate breakfast and
why his lack of clothes bothered him now he didn't know.

'What precautions are we taking?' she asked, waiting for
him to finish at the sink so she could pour bowls of water
for the dogs. Then she turned her attention to toast, as
though she was completely unaware of him.

How could she be unaware of him? he thought savagely.
He was climbing walls here! In her shorts and her tiny crop
top that left nothing to the imagination, he was so aware of
her that everything else was blotted out completely.

Like the little matter of a town threatened by bushfire.

'We're setting a safety zone up on the beach,' he managed. 'Maybe you saw…'

'There were people on the beach, setting up equipment,
as I was leaving. The safety zone's changing from the hall?'

'Yeah. This side of the river can act almost as a safety
zone by itself—it's been really well cleared. But if the fire
turns firestorm…'

'Firestorm?'

'That's what frightens us,' he told her. 'We can cope with

a fire that comes at us fast but a firestorm is something else. If it's burning so fast it starts sucking oxygen before it, then it creates its own energy. It becomes a vortex, consuming all. We'll move medical supplies down to the beach and essentials to protect a crowd. If the fire looks like escalating then everyone goes there. We'll evacuate the hospital—everyone—and we hope like hell.'

'Won't they send back-up from the mainland?' Rachel asked in a small voice, and he frowned. She sounded scared. He hadn't meant to scare her—but maybe he was a bit scared himself.

'I've been lying in bed, listening to the radio reports,' he told her. 'With this north wind after days of such heat, half the state's threatened. Every fire service is looking after its own, and the state troops are needed for the cities where most lives are at risk. So we're on our own.'

And despite the dangers the town was facing today—despite the uncertainty—he was suddenly distracted.

We're on our own.

The words jabbed deep.

He was on his own, he thought drearily as he sat on the other side of the table and ate cereal as she ate her toast. She was only feet away from him but she was so distant. So lovely.

She was married. And he had a fire to think about. Patients. Medicine. The future...

Right.

They ate on in silence, each deep in thought. And neither willing to share.

Toby arrived before they finished eating, hiking into the kitchen in his Bob-the-Builder pyjamas and blessedly breaking a tension that was well nigh unbearable.

'Hi,' he said.

'Hi, yourself.' Hugo smiled at his young son, grateful to have someone break a silence that was becoming way too difficult. Impossible. 'Breakfast?'

Toby scorned to answer such a dumb question, but his small face lit at the sight of Rachel and he launched himself onto her knees. She hugged him round the middle and he beamed.

'Can I have my toast here, Dad?'

'Why not?' Toast on Rachel's knees. If Hugo could...

No! He needed a cold shower—and he'd just had a cold shower.

He rose and made toast and handed it to his son without saying a word, while Rachel and Toby chatted like old friends.

'I need to go,' he said, more to himself than anyone else. 'Myra will be here soon.'

'Do you want me at the hospital or down at the beach?' Rachel asked, balancing her coffee around Toby's breakfast.

'Can you do standard clinic?'

She winced at that. 'Yeah, right. As if anyone's going to check in with coughs and colds today.'

'Someone needs to be there.'

She looked at him for a long moment, weighing what he'd just said. She was trying to decide whether to challenge him—whether to bring to the surface the real issue here, which was that he needed room in his head. She was infringing on that, just by being. She knew it. He needed to work alone.

'You know where to find me if you need me,' she said at last. 'Don't hesitate.'

'I won't.'

'Is the fire going to burn the town down?' Toby was sitting more firmly on Rachel's lap now, regarding his father with huge eyes. He'd claimed Rachel as his own, but he still needed his daddy.

'The fire won't burn the town,' Hugo said, and Rachel put her arms around Toby and hugged him again.

'I think today you should stay home with Myra or with me,' she told him. 'And I'm guessing Myra might want to stay on her own farm. Maybe we could pack a suitcase with all the most important things you and Daddy have. Hugo, give me a list and, Toby, you can make a list, too. Then if it gets really smoky we can take the suitcase down to the beach and we won't have to worry about the smoke making everything smell.'

'Will we take the dogs, too?'

'Of course we'll take the dogs.' She looked down at the two dogs who were slumped in soggy and sandy happiness over her feet. 'How could we let them get smoky?' She smiled up at Hugo. 'Off you go, then, Dr McInnes. Make a list and leave it for us, then you go and save the world and Toby and I will save Penelope and Digger and Toby's teddy-bear and your photo albums and whatever else we can find that's worth saving.'

'Right.'

Whatever was worth saving? Hugo made a list, which was really—stupidly—short, then made his way to the hospital. And all he could think of was...

Save me.

Christine arrived at eight-thirty to collect Toby for school and was annoyed to find he wasn't coming. 'He's staying with me for the morning,' Rachel told her, and Christine gave her a look that was meant to turn her to stone and huffed to the hospital to find Hugo.

'I went to collect the kid—'

'Toby,' Hugo said mildly. He was packing equipment

into the back of his car. He needed a full operating suite. On this day he couldn't depend on any one place to stay safe, but he could always run his car into the shallows and operate from there. If he had to. 'The kid's name is Toby.'

'Don't be stupid,' Christine snapped. 'I know what his name is. Hugo, what's going on?'

'Rachel's offered to take care of Toby. Myra wants to stay home today—understandably. Her farm's under threat as well as the rest of the town. Toby's nervous about going to school and Rachel's offered to care for him.'

'He'll be safe at school.'

Christine wasn't offering to care for Toby herself, Hugo noticed. He only had half his mind on what she was saying. The rest of his thoughts were on the contents of the cooler he was packing into his car. Did it contain every drug he could need? Had he forgotten anything important?

'So why isn't he going to school?' Christine's anger was palpable and he made himself concentrate.

'The school's happy for every child with parents available to care for them to stay home.'

'Rachel's not a parent.'

Hugo paused. He straightened and looked at Christine, really seeing her. She was brittle this morning. Tight.

'No. She's not.' He met her gaze full on.

'There's something between you and Rachel,' Christine snapped, and Hugo shook his head.

'No.'

'But you want there to be something.'

'She's married.'

'You still want there to be.'

There was only one answer to that. 'Yes,' he said gently. He paused but the thing had to be said. 'Christine, what's between us... It's happened so gradually that I've hardly noticed but it's there…the expectation that we'd start a relationship.'

'We have started a relationship.'

'No.' He shook his head. 'Christine, what's between us is no more a basis for a relationship than what was between Beth and I. I've made a mistake. Rachel… Well, it's true she's married and there's no future for us but it's made me see that you and I can never work.'

'Because you'll find someone like Rachel.'

'No.' He closed his eyes. 'I can't find anyone like Rachel. But even knowing there's someone like her in the world…it makes a difference.'

'So I've been hanging around in this one-horse dump for nothing.'

'I thought you were here for your art.'

There was a long silence. Then… 'The fire will make great pictures,' she admitted. 'And the publicity…it'll give me a market.'

'There you go, then.' He hesitated but it might as well be said. 'Be honest, Chris. That's all that's ever mattered to you—and to Beth. The art. Things. Not people.'

Silence. She half turned, ready to leave angry, but he held her with his eyes. And continued to hold.

Finally she smiled, a crooked little smile that was half mocking, half furious. 'Damn you, you know us too well. Me and Beth…'

'You love your art. People are second.'

'We could have worked out a great relationship.'

'Yeah. I practise medicine while I pay for your paints.'

She shrugged but the crooked smile stayed. 'It was worth a try.'

He shook his head. 'No. It wasn't. Christine, it's time I did things a bit differently. I think it's even time I moved on from brocade. Meanwhile, I have a fire-ravaged community to care for.'

She looked at him for a long moment and then shrugged again. A shrug of release. 'Fine. I have things to paint. But you know she'll never have you. She's married to some wealthy medical specialist in town. Why could she possibly be interested in you?'

Why indeed?

No reason at all.

Christine turned on her heel and walked away and Hugo stared after her and thought, I've just tossed in a future because of a slip of a doctor who has nothing to do with me. Nothing.

And everything.

The fire threatened for most of the morning, but that was all it did. Threaten. Reports coming into the town were that the line created by backburning was holding. The temperature soared but the wind seemed to rise to a certain velocity and stay. Holding.

Rachel worked through the myriad minor ailments presenting at the clinic. There were so many she had to concede that Hugo had been right in asking her to take over. Asthmatics were having appalling trouble with the smoke, and people who'd never had asthma in their lives had it now. The town's older residents, their capacity to retain body equilibrium with sweating compromised with age, were in real trouble. Rachel admitted two elderly men to hospital, and Don rang through wanting advice for another in the nursing home.

'The ash in the air is messing with our air-conditioning,' he told her. 'The oldies are suffering enough already and we need to have them fit to evacuate.'

'You're planning on evacuating?'

'Hugo's down on the beach, setting up a full medical centre in case,' Don told her. 'The real problems will be when this wind changes. It'll strengthen before any change and that's what Hugo's most worried about. It's what we're all worried about.'

So she should be worried, too. Rachel gave him the advice he needed, replaced the phone and looked out the window. There was nothing to see. The smoke had thickened to the stage where visibility was down to about ten yards.

Toby was settled out in the waiting room, playing with a train set. He seemed perfectly content to be there, watched over by Ruby, Hugo's receptionist, but within calling distance of Rachel. Unless she was actually examining patients, she left the door open so she could make eye contact. Every now and then he'd look up and make sure she could see him, and then he'd glance over to where the giant suitcase was sitting in a corner.

He had Rachel. He had his precious belongings. Penelope and Digger were out on the veranda, in sight. So... Hugo was out in the wide world but this link made it OK.

For now.

'Rachel!' It was a call over the intercom. Rachel had just seen her last patient but the call made her sink back into her seat. Elly, the hospital charge nurse, sounded worried. 'Rachel, are you there?'

'Yes.'

'Can you come through to the hospital? Fast? There's a baby fitting. Katy Brady, the baby's mother, is bringing her in now but she sounds as if she's unconscious already.'

A fast word of explanation—thankfully, Toby was a doctor's child and knew what the word emergency meant—and Rachel ran, leaving the dogs and Toby with Ruby. She reached the hospital entrance as a rust bucket of an ancient Ford screeched to a halt in the entrance.

'It's Connor Brady and his mother, Katy,' Elly told her as they hauled open the car door, but there was no time for more. The young mother almost fell out of the driver's seat.

The baby was slumped over his mother's knee. Katy was obviously a teenage mum—young to the point where she was scarcely out of childhood herself. She was wearing frayed jeans and a tiny crop top with tattoos peeking out from underneath. Her hair hung in dreadlocks down to her waist.

But it wasn't Katy that Rachel was looking at.

Connor Brady seemed about six weeks old and he was in dire trouble. The baby had been lying across his mother's knees and one look told Rachel what the trouble was—and what was the cause of what was happening. She put her hand on the child's forehead and winced at what she felt. Fever. The baby's temperature must be over forty.

And he was wrapped—tightly wrapped—in blankets!

'My baby…' Katy was sobbing, almost incoherent in fear, but Rachel already had him, hauling away the blankets as she lifted the little one from the car. The baby was limp, his eyes rolling back in his head as if he'd been convulsing for far too long.

'I need Dr Hugo,' the girl wailed, but Rachel wasn't listening. She was doing a fast assessment, looking for telltale signs of a meningococcal rash, checking for neck stiffness, searching…

Thankfully there was nothing.

'Get me scissors,' she told Elly. Damn, there were buttons and ribbons everywhere and she wanted these clothes off fast. There were no signs of a rash that she could see, and the little one's neck was moving freely. The likely cause of this was a simple fever combined with heat. 'Elly, run me a sink full of cool water.'

As the girl stumbled out of the car and reached for the baby. Rachel met her fear head on. 'I'm a doctor,' she told her. 'Katy, I'm pretty sure that your baby's convulsing because he's hot. We need to get him cool straight away.'

'Give him to me.' The girl was reaching out for her baby in instinctive protest at losing contact, but Rachel was already moving toward the hospital entrance, carrying the baby with her.

'Come with me,' she told Katy. 'Talk to me as I work. How long's he been like this?'

Her confident tone must have broken through. The girl hiccuped on a sob and then tried to talk.

'He's...he's got a cold. I asked Dr McInnes for antibiotics but he wouldn't give me any. Then this morning he was so stuffed up and the radio said we might be evacuated so I wrapped him up really well and started packing, but then I came back to his crib and he was...he was all rigid. Then when I picked him up he went sort of limp.'

Rachel had reached the emergency room now. She hadn't stopped—Katy had stumbled along beside her as she'd taken Connor inside. Now she had him on the examination table and was attacking the crazy layette, peeling it away like an unwanted skin. A really thick skin. Bootees, jacket, nightgown...

The baby's body was so hot.

'When you found him, did you put him straight in the car?' She was turning to the sink where Elly was already running water, but she was still questioning the frightened child by her side. The girl needed comfort but the need to establish a time frame was more urgent than comfort.

'What?'

'How long's he been fitting?' she asked directly. 'When did you phone?'

'I phoned as soon as I saw him. I picked him up and he was really odd and I was so scared I just called.' The girl hiccuped on a sob.

'The call came through eight minutes ago,' Elly told her. 'I rang you straight away.'

'How long had you left him in the cot? Could he have been fitting for a while before you found him?'

'No.' The girl was trying desperately to focus, sensing it was important. 'Just for a moment.' The last of the baby's clothes fell away to reveal a tiny limp body. 'Just two minutes at most. I wrapped him and put him down and went to get his carry-cot and then he was like this.'

So he'd been fitting for probably no more than ten minutes. But ten minutes convulsing still meant a risk of brain damage. They had to get him cool.

'What's the problem?'

It was Hugo. He'd entered unseen behind them, taking in the scene before him as he strode into the room.

'Convulsion,' Rachel said shortly, without turning. She'd lifted the baby to the sink and shoved her elbow in to check the temperature, but Elly knew her stuff. The water had the chill taken off but that was all. It was cool to the touch. Rachel lowered the little one right in, up to his neck. The remains of his clothing and all.

'Sponge water over his head,' she told Elly. 'Hugo, I need diazepam.'

He didn't question her need. 'Coming,' he replied, and disappeared.

'Come on.' The baby lay unresponsing in her hands.
Please…

It was a silent prayer, said over and over in her years

working in Emergency. Sometimes it worked. Let this be one of those times. *Please...* 'Come on, Connor.'

And, as if on cue, she felt a tremor run through the little body. Another. The baby stiffened. Arched.

Was it more of the same? A further convulsion? The eyes were still unfocused.

'I need the diazepam.'

'It's here.' Hugo was back with her. Rachel lifted the baby's slippery little body for a moment as Hugo carefully administered the drug.

Their heads bent together over the tiny child. Elly had stepped back to give Hugo room to manoeuvre. He discarded the packing, then started scooping water over the little head.

Come on. Come on.

They were willing this thing together.

And it worked. Connor's body gave a long, long shudder—and his little eyes opened. Connor stared up at the strangers above, his little mouth dropped open, his chin wobbled—and he gave a feeble, feeble wail.

It was the sweetest sound. Rachel let her breath out—how long had she been holding it? Almost since she'd seen the baby. She looked up at Hugo and saw her joy reflected in his eyes.

'He's back.'

'We have success,' Hugo said softly. 'Well done, you.'

'Lucky me,' Rachel whispered. Hugo was continuing to scoop water over the tiny, fuzzy head but the wail was building strength as young Connor realised the indignity of his position. To have this outcome was a gift. A blessing. She looked over her shoulder at the young mother. Katy was quietly sobbing, mascara running in two ugly lines down her cheeks. 'Will you hold him in the water, Katy?' she said softly. 'He sounds like he wants his mother.'

'I can't…' The girl choked on a sob. 'He shouldn't be sick. I wanted an antibiotic but Dr McInnes wouldn't give it to me. He wouldn't…' She sank down on a chair and put her head in her hands and Rachel signalled to Elly to take her place with the baby. With a questioning look at Hugo—and an answering nod—she stooped and took the girl's hands in hers, pulling them away from her tear-drenched eyes and forcing her to look at her.

'Katy, antibiotics wouldn't have helped. Connor's cold will get better all by itself. It's a combination of fever and this heat that has caused the fitting.'

'The baby book said keep him warm when he has a cold,' Katy said defiantly. 'It said it. I read…' She sniffed and tried a glare that didn't come off. 'I read everything.'

'You don't have someone who can give you advice?' Rachel frowned. 'Is there a baby clinic in town?' In the city there were clinics specifically set up for very young mothers who didn't have the support that an older woman might be capable of finding for herself.

'No.'

'There's not the staff available for a baby clinic,' Hugo said grimly from behind her. Connor's cries were escalating and he needed to raise his voice to be heard. 'I do my best but we need another doctor.' He hesitated. Then added, 'What about you? How do you feel about staying in town and helping set a baby clinic up? Plus the rest.'

'I wouldn't mind,' Rachel said before she could help herself, and suddenly she was looking at Hugo and he was looking back at her.

With unspoken thoughts…

But this wasn't the time—or the place.

'We need to move on,' Hugo said, and there was real reluctance in his voice. 'I'm sorry but we need to move fast. The fire's broken through the firebreak.'

'What does that mean?'

'That we evacuate,' Hugo told her. 'Now.'

'My baby…' Katy sobbed, and Hugo looked down at the thrashing, screaming infant and grinned.

'You know, Katy, I reckon your baby might be the least of our problems. We'll dress him in a nappy and nothing else. There's shade down at the beach. If he gets hot then you take him into the shallows. In fact, sitting in the shallows seems a fine idea for everyone. It's your job to keep Connor cool, Katy, while we look after everyone else.'

Later Rachel could only remember the next few hours as chaos. Ordered chaos, but chaos for all that. But the township had been gearing for this event for two days now and when they moved they moved fast.

Firefighting became a lower priority. Once the firebreaks had been breached everyone moved into protection mode. All firefighters were pulled out of the hills—it was pointless and dangerous to stay there. Every able-bodied person was assigned a job. Volunteers went from house to house, ensuring people had left, checking that everything that could be done had been done, then the town was left to fend for itself.

Sam Nieve was in his element. He was the elderly man with the heart condition Rachel had sent home from the fire front. Now he was in charge of what he termed the home guard. He'd taken his role very seriously—he had lists of houses with every occupant, and by the time Rachel and Hugo reached the beach, Rachel accompanying Kim's stretcher and Hugo supervising the other two seriously ill hospital inmates, he was set up at a makeshift desk, crossing off the name of every town inhabitant.

He'd even set up planking so that every person who arrived at the beach was forced to walk past his desk.

'This way I know who's still in their houses,' he told
Hugo, and there was no mistaking the pride in the man's
voice. 'There's only three I'm still worried about. Miss
Baxter, who's got a gammy leg and won't leave because
she loves her garden. Les Harding, who's worried about his
crazy feral cats. And Sue-Ellen Lesley. I've sent a couple
of teams to bring in Miss Baxter and Les and as many of
his cats as they can catch. There's only Sue-Ellen left to
worry about.'

'You didn't send a team to fetch her in?' Hugo asked.
The hospital stretchers were being set up far down the
beach. The idea was that if the fire grew to firestorm status
then people could back into the shallows. Every blanket in
the town had been collected and was already lying sodden,
waiting to cover a needy head.

Kim's stretcher had already been taken down. In a moment Rachel would go down and readjust the drips that the
girl still needed, but Hugo had stopped by Sam's desk and
so had Rachel. She saw the concern etched on Hugo's face
and was immediately worried.

'Sue-Ellen won't come if a team of people arrive,' Sam
said, casting an uncertain glance up at Hugo. 'I tried to tell
her the danger but she slammed the door in my face.'

'Have you seen her today?' Hugo asked shortly, and Sam
shook his head.

'Not since yesterday. Gary Lewis went up there last night
but she wouldn't let him in either. He's been on the radio,
worrying about her, but there's nothing I can do.'

'How did she seem?'

'Erratic. Jumpy. Angry.' The two men were looking at
each other and their worry was mirrored in each other's
eyes.

'Problem?' Rachel asked, and Hugo nodded.

'Sue-Ellen has schizophrenia. She's normally good but

something like this can throw her. I saw her last week and she was coping well but...'

'I asked if she was taking her pills,' Sam said. 'She told me to go to hell.'

'She'd say that even if she was taking them.' Hugo had turned and was staring up into the hills. As if he could see anything. The idea was ludicrous. The smoke was whirling around their faces and visibility was practically zero. The fire trucks had parked on the sand and were surrounding the temporary township in a ring—fire trucks in a semi-circle with the sea at their backs. There was safety here. But not for Sue-Ellen. 'You know she hates interference.'

'I was a mate of her dad's,' Sam said heavily. 'I know she stops taking her pills from time to time and I know it used to scare her old man.'

'Where is she?' Rachel asked.

'Out the back of the town,' Hugo said. 'She has five acres.'

'Of overgrown bush.' Sam shook his head. 'I'm not sending anyone else out there. Not now. If she won't come, she won't.'

'She might come for me.'

'Yeah, and you'll put your head in a noose because of a bloody schizo...'

But Hugo's face had set in anger. 'Sue-Ellen's a great woman.' He looked at Rachel as if he was seeking her approval. By the look on Sam's face he knew he wouldn't get approval from him. 'She used to play with the state orchestra before she became ill.'

'And now she sits up there with her damned goats, getting madder and madder,' Sam muttered, but Hugo shook his head.

'She runs angora goats. She spins and weaves and plays...'

'And talks to herself.'

'I'm wasting time.' Hugo hesitated. 'I'm the only person she trusts.'

'Where are her people?' Rachel asked, dismayed.

'Her father died five years back. She went out for a while with Gary Lewis, one of the local firemen, but she fretted that her medication was making her stupid. She made Gary leave her be, and since then she doesn't let anyone else close.'

'You can't get up there.'

'There's still time.' They turned to look northward but of course, there was nothing. An impenetrable layer of smoke. The wind was pushing ash through the air. Rachel could taste it. She opened her mouth to speak and a fine film of ash landed on her tongue. Instead of speaking, she ended up coughing.

'There's surgical masks,' Hugo said shortly. 'Get one on. You need to be fit. Rachel, I want everyone here wearing them. Can you…?'

'Can I what?' But she knew already what he was going to ask.

'Can you take over? I need to go.'

'There's Toby.' She stared at him helplessly. Myra had collected Toby when the order for evacuation had come and now Toby was splashing happily in the shallows with his mates from school. To them this was still a game. Long may that last. 'Hugo, let me go.' She placed a hand on his arm, suddenly urgent with anxiety. 'I don't have anyone. I can go.'

'You have a husband.'

'Who doesn't need me.' There, she'd said it, and even as she said it she acknowledged it was the truth. Dottie was right. 'But Toby needs you.'

'You don't know the way. And Sue-Ellen doesn't trust

you. There's no one else Sue-Ellen will come with. I'll be all right. There are dams in her home paddock. We'll make it in time.'

'Risk your life for a schizo...' Sam was bristling in indignation.

'She's not a schizo,' Hugo said wearily. 'She's a fine musician and she's a lovely person and she's my patient. I should have gone out there myself last night.' He stared helplessly at Rachel. 'I need to go. Can you cover for me here?'

Their eyes met. He knew what he was asking, she thought. He knew.

But he had to go. She knew this man well enough even after such a short time to understand that his need was absolute. Toby had an aunt. Toby had a town full of caring people.

The unknown Sue-Ellen had no one. Except Hugo.

'Of course you need to go,' she whispered, and watched his face change. 'I understand. Go, then, but go fast and only go on the understanding that you'll come back safe. Promise me?'

'I...'

'Promise?' She reached out and grasped his hands, her voice suddenly urgent. She met his eyes and hers locked with them and held. 'Hugo, you must.'

He stared down at her for a long moment and his gaze fell to their clasped hands. His mouth twisted into an expression she couldn't begin to understand.

'I promise,' he said, and he pulled her to him and kissed her hard on the lips. It was a fast and brutal kiss, a kiss born of fear and of want and of pure adrenalin. Then he was pushing her away, his eyes bleak.

'Take care of Toby,' he said as he turned and ran into the smoke. 'Keep the town safe for me until I come back.'

CHAPTER EIGHT

'HE'S got time,' Sam said uneasily. He was watching
Rachel, watching the stricken look in her eyes. He didn't
understand all of what was going on here but he understood
enough. 'The fire's coming through fast but there's no hint
of firestorm yet. If he's sensible…if the wind stays at its
current force…'

Only, of course, it didn't.

Ten minutes after Hugo had left, the wind strengthened
from strong to gale force, ripping across the crowded beach
with a force that was terrifying. The blast of hot air before
the fire was almost overpowering. Rachel was stooped over
a stretcher. Bridget McLeod had turned a hundred the week
before. The heat was making her badly dehydrated and
Rachel was setting up a saline drip. As the searing wind
blasted across the beach, the woman pushed her away.

'There's others need you more. Leave me be.'

'There's no need to be noble,' Rachel told her, trying not
to sound panicky behind her mask. 'We're organised for
this.'

She finished what she was doing and straightened, trying
to see through the swirling smoke. But the townsfolk were
prepared. A heat like this couldn't last. The gale-force wind
would blast through with frightening force but, because of
the beach, they could survive. After the initial fire front,
firefighting operations could begin again.

But for now… The little populace were hauling blankets
over their heads, following orders that had been drilled into

this fire-prone town since their childhood. Those who couldn't walk were being carried into the shallows.

'Toby.' Rachel turned to find Myra at her side. Myra had Toby in her arms with blankets wedged between them.

'There's nothing more you can do, lass. Stay with us during the worst,' Myra said, and there was no choice. Two firefighters had hold of Bridget's stretcher and were carrying her into the shallows, the old lady already covered with a soaking blanket. The rest of the stretchers were lined up where the waves broke lightly over patients' feet. Every patient had an allocated carer, each with sodden blankets.

Toby was whimpering with fear.

The noise from the fire was almost deafening.

'Take care of Toby,' Hugo had said.

Hugo.

Oh, God, Hugo...

She couldn't think of him, now. She mustn't.

The people of this tiny town were huddled in the shallows. She could scarcely breathe. There was nothing to do except survive.

Somewhere out there was Hugo.

'If I survive, so must you,' she whispered to herself as she dropped to her knees in the shallows. Toby crawled from Myra's arms to hers and clung. They had their blankets right over their heads, a sodden canopy to stop the shower of burning ash falling directly onto them. The fire was a roaring inferno. Despite the pall of smoke she could sense the flames—a wall of fire bursting down from the mountains. The air was being sucked up. The oxygen. It was so hard to breathe...

'I want my daddy,' Toby whimpered, and Rachel held him close and whispered into his hair.

'So do I,' she murmured. 'So do I. But Daddy's gone to see a patient. He'll be back soon. Please...'

*   *   *

'Sue-Ellen?' Hugo was out of the car, holding woollen wadding over his face to augment his mask as he raced toward the burning house. Vision was down to almost nothing—the fire was all around him. The trees overhead were roaring with flames.

It had caught. The back of the house had caught.

On this side of the house at least there was a little shelter. The house itself was stopping the worst of the blast. So far.

Hugo was coughing, retching. Yelling. Thinking fast. Maybe she'd gone to the dam. Maybe. It was the obvious place.

Surely she wouldn't still be in the house?

'Sue-Ellen…'

Something hit his legs—something alive. He looked down to see a half-grown collie pup whining in terror. Scratching at the door. Whining again…

Dear God.

The dog's body language was unmistakable. She was inside.

For something that had threatened for so long, it was over with a speed that was frightening all by itself. One minute the population of Cowral was crouched in the shallows while the fire blasted its way right over their heads. The next the front had moved on. The air was still choked with smoke and debris but the roaring receded. The feeling that the very air required to breathe was being sucked away was replaced by the same choking, thick sensation that had been with them most of the day.

With the passing of the front the wind dropped. The fire had made its own wind. A vortex. That's what the firefighters had said could happen and now Rachel believed them.

Toby was still cradled in her arms. Myra was beside them,

their bodies a threesome of contact with the waves splashing over them in a rhythm that had been crazily undisturbed by the fire.

Rachel pushed back her blanket and peered cautiously out.

Around her everyone was doing the same—a field of grey, sodden ghosts arising from the ashes. Katy and her baby. The ancient Bridget, hauling back her blanket herself and peering out with an interest that belied her hundred years.

Casualties?

Sam was beside her, pushing himself out from underneath something that looked like a vast eiderdown. His wife was beside him. Sylvia Nieve still had a head full of hair-rollers and as she pushed back the eiderdown she gave them a cautious pat. Making sure of what was important.

'Did everyone get to the beach?' Rachel asked, and the cold feeling of dread in the pit of her heart felt like a lump of lead.

'Elaine Baxter and Les Harding arrived just as it hit,' Ian told her. 'One of the men got bitten by one of Les's cats. The cats are here in a cage—if someone hasn't drowned them.'

'But Hugo…?' she asked.

'He didn't come back. He'll have been well into the hills when it hit.'

'Seeing his patient,' Rachel said swiftly, as Toby turned a fearful face toward Sam. She had to stay calm. Hysterics would help no one. 'There was a lady who's ill up in the hills and your daddy has gone to look after her. And I need to go, too. Toby, can you stay with Myra while your daddy and I keep on working? I'll see anyone here who needs help and then… Sam, how long do you think before we can get through to Sue-Ellen's place?'

'I'll check with the fire chief,' Sam told her.

'As soon as it's safe to move, let me know,' Rachel told him. She gave Toby a hard hug, as much to reassure herself as to reassure Toby. 'Hugo might… Hugo might need help.'

'The chief'll send a tanker.'

'I'll come, too.'

She worked solidly on the beach, coping with breathing difficulties and myriad minor injuries while she waited for the fire chief to declare it safe to travel through the town to Sue-Ellen's farmlet beyond.

'I can't believe how lightly we've got off.' The chief, a grizzled man in his fifties, pushed back his hard hat and wiped his forehead as he surveyed the clearing beach. 'The storm sucked everything up in its path but we've done such a good clearing job around the town that we've only lost four houses. And they were holiday accommodation where no one followed orders to clear.'

Once the firestorm had passed, the townsfolk streamed back to their homes in time to put out spot fires and stop the fire from taking hold. Now the main front had reached the point where land became sea. Cowral was still surrounded by a ring of fire but increasingly the town looked safe.

But Hugo…

'Can we go?' Rachel finished wrapping a burned arm with a sterile dressing. A burning branch had been flung into the shallows at the height of the fire—it must have been blown for a quarter of a mile—but the child who'd been hit was already aching to get back to the excitement. Rachel clipped the dressing, gave the boy's parents a rueful grin and turned back to the fire chief.

'You don't want to go with us, Doc,' he told her. 'I've got Gary Lewis on the truck already—he's been out on the front and when he found out Sue-Ellen didn't make it to the beach he nearly went berserk. There's one of you emotionally involved.'

'And you're not?'

He met her look square on. And sighed.

'Yeah,' he admitted. 'Of course I am.'

'Then what are we arguing over?' She was dressed in her firefighting gear. Toby was safe with Myra. There was no one else needing urgent treatment. And somewhere out there was Hugo.

She definitely needed to go.

But still the fire chief hesitated. 'Doc…'

'What?'

'You're not seeing this at its worst,' he told her. 'The river's blocked the worst of the blast here. If we were right before the front…'

She gazed at his grim face and saw the message he was trying not to tell her. 'You're telling me there's little chance Hugo's survived?'

'The boys are trying to clear the road now,' he told her. 'We'll let you know.'

'No.' She straightened her shoulders in an unconscious brace position. 'I'm a doctor. He… They may be hurt.'

His eyes met hers. Giving her the truth. 'To be honest, Doc, the chances are that they're a lot more than hurt.'

'I know. But if not… I'm bringing medical supplies and I'm coming.'

Sue-Ellen Lesley lived five minutes' drive out of town but it took two fire crews half an hour to reach it. Once outside the town boundaries there was thick bush—or what was left of thick bush. Now there was simply smouldering fire.

Eucalypts burned fast. The trees were already starting to smoulder rather than flame and the smell of burning eucalyptus oil was overpowering. Branches had dropped across the road. Trees were down. Every obstacle they reached had to be dealt with slowly—flames put out and the wood cooled enough to shift. Two fire crews worked in tandem, with a water tanker ferrying water as needed.

By the time they reached the tiny farmhouse where Sue-Ellen lived, Rachel was almost ready to scream.

'You sure you're not needed back in town?' The fire chief's face was grim as they rounded the last corner. Rachel had been working as hard as any of his team, joining the hard manual labour that had been needed to clear the road. She was working as one of his crew but there were personal issues here. He could see it. The set look on her face had him worried.

He was worried anyway. One of his boys was emotionally involved with Sue-Ellen and Gary was making himself sick with worry. And as well as Sue-Ellen… Well, this was Doc McInnes. Hell.

'If I'm needed, they'll contact me,' Rachel told him shortly. 'Elly knows where I am, and the radio network is still operational. But there's nothing back in town but heat exhaustion and dehydration, and Elly and Don and David can cope with that.'

'But—'

'Don't fight me on this,' she told him. 'We're wasting time. Just get there.'

And then the farmhouse was in view. Or what was left of the farmhouse.

Nothing.

The tiny farm cottage looked almost as if it had been vaporised—sucked into thin air with only a smouldering slab remaining where the house had once stood. Even the chimney had collapsed in on itself and was now a low mound of crumbling, smoking brick.

Nothing could have survived this.

Hugo…

Rachel caught her breath. There was a car parked beside the wreck. Or what was left of a car.

A big old family sedan.

Hugo's car.

Rachel was out of the truck before it stopped. Staring.

Her heart was somewhere else. Gone. A lifeless thing with no meaning. There were tears streaming down her face and she didn't check them. She couldn't.

Hugo.

And then a shout. From Gary, the giant of a young fire-fighter who was so worried about Sue-Ellen.

'Over here. He's over here. In the dam.'

Gary, who obviously knew the lie of the land, had spared not even a glance for the burnt-out shell of the house where it was obvious nothing could have survived, but he'd moved swiftly toward a bank over to the left. Now he stood on the rise and yelled back to them.

'They're over here. They're in the dam. Doc with about thirty bloody goats and a dog and Sue-Ellen. They're alive.'

Hugo was alive, but Sue-Ellen barely qualified. He'd heard them come but he could do nothing. The girl in his arms needed all his attention. Her eyes were wide but what she was seeing was invisible to him. She was drifting in and out of consciousness. Her blood pressure was way down and her pulse was thready and weak.

He needed equipment. He needed help.

The grass at the verge of the dam was still smouldering. He couldn't move.

So he lay, supporting Sue-Ellen, partly submerged in the water. Beside them, her half-grown collie lay and whined and whined, and around them Sue-Ellen's beloved angora goats shifted in anxiety.

The girl in his arms stirred and seemed to focus. 'I...can't...' she whispered.

'You don't need to do anything, Sue-Ellen,' he told her, trying hard to keep his voice reassuring and steady. 'You've done it all. Your goats are fine. You've saved your pup. You're burned but not too badly. You'll be OK. People are coming. We'll both be looked after. Your goats. Your dogs. All of us.'

She was no longer listening. She'd dropped again into unconsciousness.

He closed his eyes and when he opened them Rachel was slithering down the bank toward him.

His Rachel.

'I haven't been able to help. I haven't had anything to work with,' Hugo told her. The fire crew had laid a thermal blanket over the mud at the side of the dam. Gary—appalled beyond belief—had lifted Sue-Ellen's limp body from Hugo's grasp and laid her tenderly on the bank. Someone else had run for Rachel's equipment. Now they were working fiercely in tandem.

Severe burns. Shock. Smoke inhalation. Why hadn't they been able to get here earlier? Rachel thought fiercely as she checked blood pressure. Eighty over fifty. Hell.

'Gary, look after Hugo,' she ordered. As one of the few professional firefighters, Gary would know basic first aid, but Hugo was having none of it. He brushed Gary aside and reached for the IV equipment.

'I'm fine. I haven't been able to help but I can now.'

'Are your hands burned?'

'No.'

'Your voice is rasping.'

'I'm not burned. It's just from smoke inhalation.'

'Well, then…'

'Leave it.'

She cast a doubtful glance at him but his look was grim and determined. She had the sense to let it be, moving to Sue-Ellen's mouth, tilting her chin so her jaw dropped open.

'I checked,' Hugo said briefly. 'There's no obvious burns to her mouth. The pharynx isn't swollen.'

'Lucky.' Rachel placed a stethoscope on Sue-Ellen's chest while Hugo accepted the bag of saline from Gary and swabbed the girl's bare arm. IV access would have to be ante-cubital—through the elbow—because of deep burns on her hands. She was still deeply unconscious.

'Oh, God, she's dying,' the young firefighter whispered, and Rachel found time to glance up at him.

'You sound like you love her,' she said gently, and the young giant nodded. They were working together to rip away clothing and place the bags of saline.

'We used to go out with each other. When she was diagnosed with schizophrenia she called it off. Said it was unfair to me. I came around last night to see if she needed help and she told me to clear off. But she didn't want me to. I could tell. And then today I was caught out with the fire truck and couldn't check. Hell. I didn't know… I didn't know…'

He hadn't known how much he loved her, Rachel thought, with the sudden insight of someone who'd been down just that road.

'She'll be right,' she said gently. 'Gary, can you find us more blankets from the truck? I know it's crazy but the water will have chilled her and we need her warm. You'll find the sheets I brought—they look like a cross between

plastic and tin foil. And I have sheets of clingwrap. I wan
them, too.'

The firefighter nodded, grateful to do anything. Anything
He disappeared at a run.

'We need to contact air ambulance services,' Hugo sai
in a voice that was growing more ragged by the minute.

'I already have.' It was the fire chief, appearing over th
dam bank with his radio receiver still in his hand. 'One o
the state's medical evacuation helicopters is available
Apparently our firestorm has upgraded us. Cowral's becom
a priority and the chopper will be here in twenty minutes.

'If we can keep her alive,' Hugo muttered, and Rache
shook her head.

'There's no doubt.' She had an oxygen mask on the girl'
face and already Sue-Ellen's complexion was deepening un
der the grime to something that looked more healthy. As i
on cue, the girl stirred and moaned.

'Morphine,' Rachel murmured, reaching behind her fo
her bag, but it was Hugo who administered it. He wa
shocked and battered but he was working on autopilot.

'Let me go. Let me go…' It was a thready whisper bu
she was starting to fight them.

'Haloperidol?' Rachel queried, and Hugo nodded. I
Sue-Ellen was schizophrenic then the whole combination o
events might well be enough to push her over the edge
Sedation was imperative.

The fluids were flowing freely now. Rachel took anothe
blood-pressure reading and breathed a bit more easily.

'A hundred and ten, seventy. See, Hugo? We'll do it.'

'You'll do it,' he muttered. 'I couldn't do it without you
Hell, Rachel, I had nothing.'

'Because your car went up in flames,' she said brusquely
'It could be said you had an excuse. I don't think the med

ical board is going to strike you off for losing your doctor's
bag. And you did save the patient.'

Gary arrived back, sliding down the bank with a bunch
of blankets. He looked worried sick.

'Let's find the extent of these burns,' Hugo said. He was
starting to sound in control a bit—just a little. He lifted
Sue-Ellen's palms and grimaced. Rule of palm… Take the
area of a size of a palm print and measure how many palm
prints were burned on the girl's body. Twenty? Thirty? They
were looking at something like thirty per cent burns.

'We need that fluid coming in fast.'

'We have it,' Rachel replied.

'Have we got dressing packs?'

'We have everything we need.' She'd carried her bag
with her, and she flipped it open. As Hugo started gently
separating burned fingers—imperative in these first few
minutes—she started sorting, handing Hugo sachets of specially formulated gel to soak the burns, then gauze to place
over them before they wrapped the whole area in clingwrap.
It was imperative to get the area sterile and air-free.

At what cost came the time spent in the dam? What in-
fections were in the ash- and mud-laden water? But at least
it meant she had a chance.

And a chance was what she most needed. As Gary
stooped over Sue-Ellen and her eyes fluttered open and
found Gary…as Gary lifted her hand to his face and
held…just held, Rachel thought Sue-Ellen had everything
she needed right here. Right now.

She was injured almost to death.

But she had her love and one look at Gary told her that
it would take more than schizophrenia or bushfires to part
them again.

And all of a sudden Rachel was blinking back tears.
Of…envy?

*   *   *

'She was in the house.'

Hugo was sitting in the mud on the dam bank, his head in his hands. Behind them the whirr of the helicopter was fading into the distance.

They'd lifted Sue-Ellen from the dam bank, warmed her shocked body, covered her burns with antiseptic gel and the thin plastic burn wrap and continued her on intravenous fluids. They'd given her as much morphine as they could. Then they'd loaded her into the medical evacuation helicopter where a team of skilled medicos were waiting to take her to Sydney.

Gary had gone, too. It hadn't been discussed.

She had every chance of survival, Rachel thought as she watched the chopper disappear into the distance. Although the burns to her legs and hands were too extensive to be treated in a small country hospital, they shouldn't be extensive enough to be life-threatening. Not with the prompt treatment she'd had and the fact that in an hour she'd be in the best burns unit in the state.

And the schizophrenia? With love and devotion she had a good chance of a stable life. Gary wasn't about to be pushed aside again, for however noble a motive, Rachel thought.

And here... Already the goats were emerging from the water, starting to forage over burned ground. Amazingly, they even looked as if they were finding things to eat.

The goats might be back to business as usual but Hugo wasn't. He was sitting on the dam bank, looking sick. Rachel sat down beside him, hauled Pudge, Sue-Ellen's pup, up onto her knee and held the shaking dog. With her free hand she took Hugo's and held that, too. Tight.

'Hugo...'

He looked dreadful. While they'd worked over Sue-Ellen

he'd been efficient, doctor in medical mode, but as the chopper left the fight seem to have drained out of him.

'Hugo,' she whispered again, and he stirred, as if trying to rouse himself from a dreadful dream.

'The house had started to burn before I reached her,' he said at last, wearily, as if hardly conscious that Rachel was beside him. 'She must have gone back in. I yelled out and I could hear her inside the house, screaming for Pudge. Screaming. But Pudge was outside. The pup came to greet me as I pulled up, desperate. As if he knew his mistress was inside.'

'So you went in.'

'Of course.' He winced and Rachel looked down at the hand she was holding. There were blisters there. Burns. He'd been wearing protective clothing and that was intact, but there were spot burns on his hands and on his face.

He'd been through hell.

She pulled back on her hand, afraid she was hurting him, but his grip tightened.

'But you found her,' she said softly, and he nodded.

'I found her in the back bedroom and the curtains were burning. The window had exploded inward. And she had bare feet. Bare feet!'

'Hugo—'

'I should have come last night. I should have thought of Sue-Ellen then.' He groaned. 'Hell, I should have—'

'You're one man,' she said gently.

'I went to the beach.'

'There was no danger last night. And other people checked. Gary loved her and he checked. She sent him away. There was nothing else you could do. You know that.'

'But today—'

'Today you came. You came in time. They're saying on the beach that Sue-Ellen refused to evacuate. Do you think

she would have evacuated if you'd ordered her to? You're
not omnipotent, Hugo. You're human. You're a doctor and
a really fine one at that, but you're still human.' She took
his palms into her hands and looked down. He was burned
but not too badly. Still… Her face twisted. Dear God, he'd
come so close. 'You're a lovely, lovely man,' she whispered. 'The best… Oh, God, Hugo if I'd lost you…'

He wasn't hearing. He was still with Sue-Ellen.

'I thought she was stable,' he said bleakly. 'Sensible. Last
time I saw her… I was out here three days ago when the
fires first threatened. She talked about evacuation plans. So
why didn't I check?'

'Because you can't be everything to everyone,' she said
softly. Then, because she couldn't bear to watch the pain in
his eyes any more, she took his face in her hands and kissed
him—softly, on each eyelid in turn. 'Sue-Ellen made her
own decision not to leave her animals. That's her responsibility. Back at the beach… Sam called her a schizo—a
mental case—and if that's the way you regarded her then
yes, you were responsible for her because she wasn't responsible for herself. You should have locked her up and
taken total control. But you said she was a person capable
of her own decisions.'

'Yes, but—'

'But nothing.' Rachel's voice was urgent now. She could
see the self-loathing in Hugo's eyes and she wasn't having
any of it. He was hurt, this man. She could put bandages
on his hands but it wasn't enough. What hurt more than a
heart?

'Sue-Ellen knew the dangers. Sam and Gary both said
she'd been warned. She chose to stay.'

'She was ill.'

'Would you have locked her in a mental institution?'

'No, but—'

'But nothing. Sue-Ellen lived independently and she was hurt, making that life for herself. I won't have you blaming yourself, Dr McInnes.'

He looked up at her, and the beginning of an exhausted smile crossed his face. Just a trace.

'Bossy, aren't we?'

'It's what I do best,' she said softly, and smiled back at him.

Hugo gazed up at her. Really looked. His burned hand came up and brushed the curls from her face. They were tumbling every which way from under her hard hat.

She'd be smoke-grimed, she thought—black with soot and sand and smoke. But Hugo's eyes were holding her and his fingers traced her cheekbone gently—a feather touch.

'You're so beautiful.'

'Beautiful and bossy?' she asked in a voice that wasn't quite steady.

'That's the one. Rachel...'

'What?'

'I need to kiss you,' he told her.

And what was a girl to say to a request like that?

She kissed him.

More than that, she gave her heart. Right there and then.

Or maybe it had been given in those awful moments on the beach, under the sodden blanket with the fire roaring overhead, thinking that somewhere out here was Hugo. Her love...

Her love.

There was another love. Craig. That hadn't disappeared—it never could. There was still commitment, still pain, but it didn't stop this flowering that was happening within her right now.

Dottie had said it was time she moved on. Put Craig behind her. But it wasn't like that. She hadn't been able to put Craig behind her for eight long years.

And she couldn't now. She didn't need to.

Because Craig was still with her. Craig was a part of who she was, a part of her loving. She held Hugo's dear, scorched face in her hands and she kissed him with all the love in her heart and she knew that this was no betrayal.

This was an extension of loving. A wealth of love. Broadening, expanding her heart, to take in Toby and Cowral and Penelope and Digger and Sue-Ellen and maybe a few crazy goats clustered around and a confused pup called Pudge.

And Hugo.

She kissed him and found herself melting. Not just her lips. Her whole life, melting away and reforming. Regrouping. Stronger, richer, deeper.

Love...

He tasted of fire. He tasted of heat and want and aching need.

He tasted of... Hugo.

Her fingers held him, curled into his hair, clinging, letting his mouth devour her, knowing that for him this kiss was as affirmation of life as well as love.

Knowing for him this was the only way to move forward. Through love.

Love was...here. Love was now.

Love was Hugo.

There was no time for each other. Not now.

They held each other for as long as they could, desperately taking what they most needed from this precious contact. But, of course, there was more needed of them this day than the care of Sue-Ellen.

The fire chief stood behind them and coughed and waited.

He'd given them space. He was a wise man and he'd seen their need. He'd directed his team away from them as the chopper left and had given them as much time as he could, but needs were breaking through.

'Doc…' He coughed a couple of times and tried again. 'Doc…'

They broke apart. Sort of. Battered and filthy, they sat in the mud and looked up at him, and the fire chief gave them a grin which said the incongruous picture they made was hardly lost on him.

'Geez, whatever turns you on, Doc,' he said to Hugo. 'Me, I like my missus in a sexy negligee but if you like 'em covered with soot—well, each to his own. But kinky is what I call it.'

Rachel blushed. She blushed from the roots of her hair to the tips of her toes and she tried to haul away, but Hugo was having none of it. His hand tightened around her waist and he grinned.

'Sexiest lady I know.'

'Isn't she just.' The fire-chief's grin broadened. 'We'll have her up on our calendar next year, hard hat included. Look, I'm sorry to disturb you…'

'You'd think we could have a bit of privacy,' Hugo complained. He seemed suddenly almost jovial. 'We've searched so hard to find it. And here we are with only thirty goats, one dog and twenty odd firefighters as an audience.' His smile faded, just a bit, but it didn't leave his eyes completely. 'Don't tell me. Problems?'

'No major ones.' The chief wiped his eyes with the back of his hand and something suspiciously like moisture smeared his cheek. 'We've been so bloody lucky. It's amazing. But…'

'But?'

'One of the teams down at the river are saying some of

the guys are suffering from smoke inhalation. And the pub lican's wife…she tried to hook up the hose as the first o the heavy smoke hit the town but she was working blind and she fell over the tap. She sounds like she's broken her toe.'

A broken toe…

'Is that all?' Hugo asked in voice that was none too steady.

'That's all, Doc,' the chief told him. 'For now. You guys might have time to continue this…discussion later if you need to. But for now I'm afraid Cowral wants you both to be doctors.'

Hugo smiled and turned back to Rachel. To his love. 'Can we be doctors for a bit?' Hugo asked her. He held Rachel close and the expression in his eyes told her all she ever needed to know about this man. There was no need for anything else. Just Hugo. His feel. His touch. His eyes.

And the way he looked at her.

'What do you think, my love?' he whispered. 'Can we be doctors for a bit?'

'As long as we stay being more than just doctors under-neath,' she answered, her eyes smiling and holding and lov-ing. 'As long as we stay just as we are.' And then her smile broke into a chuckle of love and laughter and joy. 'Only maybe a little bit cleaner.'

They worked then, through the rest of that long, long day. Because, of course, it wasn't just firefighters with smoke inhalation and Maddie Forsyth's broken toe. The town was in firefighting mode. There were minor burns everywhere. Exhaustion. Dehydration. Stress.

Hugo and Rachel worked together and separately. They saw an endless stream of patients, one after another. The little hospital was a clearing-house through which most of the town's population passed at some time during the day.

Toby was there from time to time, brought in by Myra just to see that Daddy and Rachel were still there. Still fine.

Toby and Myra came with three dogs. Because of course they couldn't leave the shaky Pudge at the farm. Hugo had scooped him up and carried him into town beneath his fire-crew jacket and had handed him over to Myra to fuss over. Amazingly, the two big dogs seemed to sense the little dog's distress and now Pudge was the centre of a two-dog, house-keeper and small boy circle of protection. By his second visit into the hospital the puppy's tail was starting to wag again.

'I'll telephone Melbourne and tell them to pass the news on to Sue-Ellen,' Hugo told Rachel as Myra herded her charges outdoors again. 'It'll do her more good than medi-cine.'

In the middle of all this...he could find time to think laterally about Sue-Ellen. That was what country practice was all about, Rachel thought as she returned to washing ash out of a firefighter's eyes. Country practice was medi-cine from textbooks—plus the rest.

It was healing—just for her.

They worked far into the night. The townsfolk had gone home from the beach. The wind died, and about ten o'clock the hoped-for change blew through softly from the south. The air temperature dropped to almost cool and there was a spattering of blessed rain.

But still they worked. A team had been organised to go from house to house, checking, not for spot fires now but on people's health. The elderly and those at risk had had a day where they'd been tested to the limit. They could go home now and maybe collapse with exhaustion, stress, smoke inhalation, minor injuries...

So everyone was checked. Cowral looked after its own. And as each problem was reported, it was passed on to the medical team.

At two a.m. Rachel finally arrived back in the kitchen of the doctors' residence. Myra had taken Toby and all three dogs out to her place for the night. There were casseroles sitting on the kitchen table—of course—but Rachel was beyond eating. She sat and stared at nothing. At nothing at all.

And fifteen minutes later Hugo walked in.

He was as exhausted as she was. He appeared at the screen door and his face was grey with fatigue. She rose and looked at him. Just...looked. And what passed between them...

It was a vow. It was confirmation of all they had come through that day.

It was the start of their life together.

'Rachel,' he said at last, and it was as if it was a blessing.

'Hugo,' she whispered, and walked straight into his arms.

There was no time then for anything but love.

There was no time for talking. No time for anything but filling this aching, searing need. Holding. Finding their rightful place.

They showered together because to do otherwise was to waste time. Their filthy clothes were shed together—clothes that on any day but this one would have had both doctors struck off the medical register as disgraces to the medical profession. But no one had minded their clothes. They'd been doctors first and foremost. They'd seen to the town's medical needs.

But now...the need was past. The town's needs.

There was time now for their own needs.

Time to become lovers.

There was no hesitation. No questions. There were only answers.

Their bodies met in joyful wonder. They washed each other under the stream of warm water, soaping, smiling, learning each other's bodies in this, the most intimate act of cleaning. Soaping off the layers of grime to reveal bodies that were already known and loved.

His hands were smoothing the soap over her skin and it was the most erotic of sensations. She had the flannel and was rubbing his back, but her body was falling forward, leaning into him, letting her mouth touch his…

Tasting. Wanting.

Needing!

The need was mutual. All-exclusive.

It was as if this man and this woman had been meant for each other—destined—from the beginning of time.

And then they were together in Hugo's big bed, dry and warmed but still naked, gloriously naked. Skin against skin, holding, holding, narrowing the gap, merging…

Man and woman becoming one.

It had been so long.

Had it ever been this good? Rachel didn't know. She couldn't think. She couldn't compare. What had been between Rachel and Craig was another time. Another life. It had been precious—was still precious—but it was a thing apart.

This was now. This man, her beloved Hugo, holding her as if he loved her.

He did love her. She knew it and she gloried in it.

Craig would not gainsay her this love. Because she loved Craig she knew, with a surety that was a part of her own heart, that she had his blessing. She could feel it.

Her body was doubly blessed.

Dear heaven, the feel of Hugo. The wonder. His big hands were holding her as if she was the most precious thing in the world. His warmth, the smell of him, the taste…

The way her body moulded around him. Opened. Welcomed. He came into her, and their mutual need was overwhelming. The wonder…

The joy.

They slept. How could they not sleep after this day? Their exhaustion was absolute. Sated with loving, they slept entwined, and Rachel fell into a sleep as deep as she'd ever been in.

Ever since the accident—ever since that dreadful day— her sleep had been troubled, disturbed, as if she'd had to stay awake for the next disaster. There would be another disaster. Her world had been pulled from under her feet and she couldn't trust.

She couldn't sleep.

But now…in this man's arms, she slept. Let tomorrow bring what it may. For now there was only this man and his arms and his body and his love.

And Hugo?

It had never been like this with Beth. He'd drifted into marriage with Beth as he'd nearly drifted into marriage with her sister. Stupid. Stupid, stupid.

Yet how could he have known it had been stupid? He'd never known it could be like this. He woke about dawn and his fingers twined gently through Rachel's tumbled curls. How could he have suspected there was loving like this in the world?

This wonderful woman. This…blessing.

She stirred in sleep, her eyes half opened and she smiled

at him. His heart twisted inside him and he gathered her to him with such tenderness. The most precious thing…

Rachel.

Her eyes closed and she snuggled into him. Her breasts moulded to him. He felt desire stir, but exhaustion was still there. Desire could wait, he thought with a growing joy. It could wait an hour or two. There was all the time in the world. This was his Rachel. Rachel…

Murmuring her name into her hair, he drifted back to sleep.

The phone woke them.

It was late. At least eight. The sun was streaming across the brocade quilt. He'd get rid of it, Hugo thought, and then joyously, yes! He'd get rid of every piece of brocade in the house.

This day was the first day of the rest of his life. His life with Rachel.

She was waking beside him, her eyes fluttering open, smiling, reaching up to touch his unshaven chin.

The phone was ringing.

Rachel.

Medical imperative. Answer the phone. He smiled back at her and then answered the phone.

A woman's voice, urgent with need.

'Is Rachel there? Dr Harper? She's not answering her cellphone. I need to speak to her.'

'Sure.' He heard the fear and reacted. His eyes sent Rachel an urgent message and handed her the phone.

Rachel took the receiver and listened.

'Dottie.'

She was suddenly wide awake, pushing herself up in bed, oblivious of the fact that she was naked. A sunbeam was streaming across her creamy breasts.

Dear God, she was beautiful!

But her voice sounded concerned.

'No, Dottie, we're fine. I'm sorry. I should have rung you last night. I might have known you'd see it on the news reports. No. The town's been left basically intact. We're safe.'

'No.'

'No.'

Then her voice softened with dread. 'But he can't… Dottie, he was stable…'

She listened some more and then put her lips tightly together. Her eyes closed as if in pain.

'Of course I'll come,' she whispered. 'Of course. Just as soon as I can get there.'

The line went dead. Hugo lifted the receiver from Rachel's suddenly limp grasp and laid it back on the cradle. Then he turned and took her hands in his.

'What is it, Rachel?'

She opened her eyes and stared at him but she wasn't seeing him. She was seeing something a long way away. In the far, far distance.

'It's Craig,' she whispered.

'Craig?'

'My husband. He's dying.'

CHAPTER NINE

SOMEHOW, while Hugo helped Rachel put her belongings together and practically force-fed her toast and arranged for someone to drive her…somehow he got it out of her.

'Craig and I were in a car smash eight years ago,' she said, her voice laced with pain. 'We were med students together. We'd gone out together since school. Dottie, Craig's mum, is practically my mum. We were so close. We got married and everything was perfect and then some drunk driver smashed into us on a blind bend when we were coming home from one of Craig's football matches. The drunk was on the wrong side of the road and there was nothing Craig could do to avoid him. I was hurt. Craig… Craig was hardly touched. Except for a blow to his head. One blow. One blow and he was unconscious. And he never woke up.' Her voice broke on a sob and Hugo held her mug of tea to lips that were tight with the shock of past hurt and hurt still to come.

'So Michael… The guy at the dog show?'

'He's a schmuck,' she said. 'Dottie said I should get away. Have some fun. And I met you.'

He took a deep breath. Did some fast thinking. Last night he'd made love to a woman he'd thought was in an unhappy marriage. Now…

Things had changed. She'd changed.

And his head… He was having trouble getting it around this.

But the pain on her face was real and dreadful and it needed to be addressed now.

'Rachel, I'm really sorry.'

She pulled herself together then. Sort of. 'Sorry? I'm not.' She gave him a fleeting, hurting smile. 'How could I be sorry for last night? It was the most wonderful…' Her voice broke, but she managed to go on. 'Hugo, it was fantastic. The best. I could never, ever regret it. But you do see that I need to go.'

'Of course you do.' It tore him apart that he couldn't put her in his car and drive her to Sydney himself but, of course, he couldn't. The town still had medical imperatives.

At least the road was open. Rain in the night had cleared the route out of town. He'd put out a call and someone would drive her all the way to Melbourne. He could arrange that at least.

But he couldn't leave.

'Rachel…'

'I know.' She swallowed the last of her tea and stood, looking down into the dregs at the bottom of the mug. 'I know. I'm sorry, Hugo. I'm sorry, love…'

Hugo worked for that day—long hours of minor crises. He worked the next. The day after that…

The day after that he could bear it no longer. He talked to Myra and to Toby, contacted a locum service and found some help and went to town.

The thin blue line rose and fell. Rose and fell. Rose and fell.

How long does love last?

The young woman sat and watched as she'd sat and watched for years.

'I love you, Craig,' she whispered, but there was no answer, as there'd never been an answer.

Dappled sunlight fell over lifeless fingers. Beloved eyes, once so full of life and laughter, stayed closed.

The blue line rose and fell. Rose and fell.

Faltered.

'I love you, Craig,' she whispered again, and blessed his face with her fingers. 'My love…'

How long does love last?

Maybe for no longer than a breath?

Hugo stood at the ward door and watched Rachel. She was sleeping. Her bright curls were tangled on the white coverlet. Her hand held his. Her face rested on his chest.

Hugo's eyes moved to the monitor and stilled. The heartbeat was fast and irregular. He watched.

He'd learned so much over the last few days. Questions that should have been asked of Rachel had been answered by the consultant he'd called.

'Eight years in a coma. He was a strong young man, Hugo, with nothing but a bleed into the brain to maim him. We thought he could live even longer than this. There's been no end in sight. But a few months ago he suffered a clot…'

'Deep vein thrombosis?'

'You know it's not uncommon in cases like this. The body's so inactive… We thought maybe we'd lose him then. I think his parents and Rachel said their goodbyes. But he rallied. And Rachel went on waiting.'

'Rachel…'

'I've known Rachel since she was a medical student,' the consultant said bluntly. 'She and Craig were a great pair—lovely creatures with the world at their feet. Since the accident it's as if someone's blown Rachel's flame out. She's clever, she's an extraordinary doctor but every night she sits by Craig's bedside and she simply…well, she simply is.'

'She must have loved him.'

'It's so hard to move forward,' the consultant said gently. 'Without a death. Dottie and Lewis, Craig's parents, well, after the clot they seemed to let go. They pushed Rachel. She was making the first tentative steps. And now… The clots have reappeared. One's sitting in his lung. This is the end, Hugo. The end of a very long story.'

So now Hugo stood at the door and watched her. He simply…watched her.

As she'd watched Craig for all these years.

With all the love in her heart.

She'd gone for coffee.

It had been one hell of a day. The emotions in Rachel's tired mind were threatening to overwhelm her. How could this happen? While she was falling in love—for the second time—her first love was deciding to slip away from this world.

She didn't feel guilty. She couldn't. How could she? In a sense it was because of Craig that she'd fallen so heavily for Hugo. The love she felt for both men was mixed up, intertwined.

Because she loved Hugo, her love for Craig couldn't die, regardless of what happened to the man in the bed. The man she'd loved for ever.

But she couldn't think of Hugo now. He was still there in the background—a warmth and a joy in the back of her mind, a vast tenderness that filled the cold and the emptiness that had been with her for so long.

But for now there was only Craig. His breathing had become shallow. There was a pneumonia that wouldn't clear. It was his time.

Time to let go.

She filled her coffee-mug in the relatives' kitchenette at

the end of the ward and walked slowly back to the small room where Craig lay by himself. And stopped short in the doorway.

Hugo was there. Hugo was sitting in the chair beside Craig's bed and he was speaking.

'Mate, I have no idea whether you can hear me. The jury's out on brain injury—on this dying business. How much you know. How much you can sense. But I figured...the way I felt I had to come. I had to talk to you. You have the right.'

Rachel stepped back. He hadn't heard her return. She leaned against the wall of the corridor and she closed her eyes. And listened while Hugo spoke to Craig.

While one love spoke to another.

'I don't know how much Rachel has told you, but I'm Hugo McInnes. I'm a country family doctor. I'm a widower, with a kid and a dog, and I'm thirty-five years old. And I'm in love with your wife.'

And I'm in love with your wife. It was such a bold statement that Rachel drew in her breath. She swallowed. And she waited.

'It sounds pretty dreadful, doesn't it?' Hugo said, and paused. 'I never thought I'd say that to someone I think of as a friend. That I'm in love with your wife. But maybe it's because that's the way I think of you that I can say it. As a friend.'

There was a long pause then. Out in the corridor Rachel set her coffee-mug down on the floor. Her fingers were trembling. A couple of nurses walked past and looked at her in concern but she waved them on.

He'd come...

'Craig, you and Rachel have loved each other for a long time. I know that.' Hugo's voice was soft but pervasive, reaching where she strained to hear. 'I know that. I can see it in Rachel's eyes. I can see how deep your love was. After all this time…part of Rachel is you. Well, now I've fallen for her—fallen for her in a big way, maybe as hard as you ever fell. But, of course, it's different. I'm not loving a girl straight out of school. I'm loving a woman who's been loved before—who's loved before. Who's become what she is because some guy a long time ago made her smile. Lit up her world. Took her in his arms and loved her and made her feel that anything was possible when love was around.'

Hugo hesitated, as though finding difficulty in finding words. The right words. But somehow he kept going.

'I've never felt like that,' he said at last. 'I drifted into a marriage that was a bit of a disaster. My wife died and that made me feel even more self-contained. Like love—married love—was something you read about in romance novels. Not something that changed the world. Only then I met Rachel.'

Another silence. Then…

'She's really something,' he whispered. 'She's the best. You and Rachel must have been amazing. And what Rachel's grown to be…because of you…

'You know,' he said, his voice still soft, 'that's why I'm here. To tell you that you're a part of Rachel. And because of that… I guess you'll be a part of our family. You'll be with us. You'll live on.'

Rachel's eyes were filling with tears. She lifted a finger and wiped them away but more followed. Still he spoke.

'It sounds corny, doesn't it?' Hugo was saying ruefully. 'Lives on for ever in our hearts. It's true, though. I've finally figured this love thing out. The more you have the more you seem to get. The more you give, the more it grows around you. Because you loved Rachel and she loved you…she's reached out and she's enveloped us. Me. My kid—did I tell you that? I have a six-year-old called Toby who thinks your Rachel is the best thing since sliced bread. Rachel's promised to teach him to kick a football. She says you taught her that. Your football…living on in my kid.

'And there's more.' He was smiling. Rachel could hear it in his voice. 'We have a couple of dogs. Digger—he's mine. He's a mutt. And there's Penelope. She belonged to some creep we met and didn't like. I'm about to give the guy an offer he can't refuse because our family's too small. We need at least two dogs. We have another—Pudge— who's staying with us while someone else we know and love recovers from an injury. There'll be more. Rachel is the sort of woman who'll keep an open door to strays, and I'm with her there. And there'll be kids.'

Rachel drew her breath in at that. The tears dried. She was smiling. Stupidly she was grinning. The nurses passed her again and she grinned at them like a fool and they looked at her like she was demented.

It didn't matter. What had he said?

How could she forget? *There'll be kids.*

'We'll have babies,' Hugo said softly. 'At least, I hope like hell we'll have babies. I haven't actually discussed this with Rachel yet but, hey, this is the equivalent of girls' talk with a bloke. We can say anything in here, right? Right. Well, having babies… Before Toby was born I thought one was enough, but he's twisted himself round my heart like you wouldn't believe. And if it was Rachel's kid… Your kid…'

Out in the corridor Rachel drew in her breath once again.

'You see, there's the thing,' Hugo said apologetically. 'Because if we have another kid then I'm going to be think- ing that he, or she, is part of you. Any baby we have would seem your gift to us. You've given me the gift of love. The gift of Rachel. I'll never forget it, mate. I'll never forget you. You'll be held in our family in all honour. If we have a boy then there's no doubt what he'll be called. I'm not sure how we can swing Craig into a girl's name...' Rachel heard the smile in his voice. 'Maybe we'll just have to keep on trying until we get a boy. It'd be fine with me. As long as it's fine by you.'

Rachel's eyes were closed. The emotions surging around her heart were threatening to overwhelm her. She leaned hard against the wall—she needed its support to stop herself falling over. It seemed as if the whole world had stopped breathing. The silence went on for ever. And then...

'Well, that's all I wanted to say,' Hugo murmured. 'I needed to get that off my chest. You've got things to do. Breathing to concentrate on.' Rachel peeped forward and saw Hugo's hand lift Craig's and hold it. Two big hands, men's hands, intertwined. It was all she could do not to cry out at the sight of it. Her breathing started again, ragged and filled with tears.

'And you have dying to face,' Hugo whispered. 'I'm sorry, mate, that you can't live. I'm that damned sorry—and if giving up Rachel's love would bring you back to us I'd do it in a minute. But the guys in consultant suits are telling me it won't happen. So I'll say goodbye. I'll leave you to your parents and to Rachel. But know... Know, mate, that in our house—in any home that I'm lucky enough to build and share with your wife—you'll be honoured and you'll be loved for ever.'

It was five minutes before Hugo left the ward. When he came out into the corridor there was no one to be seen.

Just a mug of cold coffee lying abandoned on the polished floor.

CHAPTER TEN

ASHES to ashes. Dust to dust.

The wind blew gently across the mountain graveyard. Rachel stood silent as the coffin was lowered into the waiting ground. Lewis and Dottie stood on either side of her, holding her, united in a grief that had been agonised and raw eight years ago but was now muted—a soft and wondrous goodbye. These three who still loved Craig. Who would always love Craig.

In the end, it was good. This tiny graveyard… It was near to the place where Craig had been born—a tiny country cemetery where the wind keened around the mountains and a man could see for miles.

Where spirits could at last be free.

This was a good place for Craig to come to rest. His grandparents, his great-grandparents, a babe who would have been Craig's brother if he'd been born at term…they were all here.

His body was where it belonged and Craig lived on in those who loved him.

Rachel hugged those holding her—this man and this woman who'd been by her side for so long.

'It's OK,' she whispered, and Dottie smiled through her tears.

'It surely is.' Dottie blinked back tears and looked across at her husband—and Lewis released Rachel and came around to take his wife in his arms.

'Well done, lass,' Lewis said. He was a big gruff man who'd loved his son with an intensity that was even greater than his passion for the football he'd once played. He hugged his wife but he looked over her head at Rachel. 'And now it's time for you, girl, to move on.'

'Move on…'

'Your young man.' Lewis kissed his wife gently on the top of her head and then Dottie and Lewis both turned and smiled at her. 'Your Hugo.'

'My Hugo?'

'He's here,' Lewis said, and motioned out to the road where the track led down the mountain to the tiny township below. And there was Hugo. He was standing by his car. He didn't approach the mourners. He simply stood. Waiting.

'He's here,' Lewis said simply. 'It's time you went to him.'

Rachel closed her eyes, and when she opened them they were smiling at her. Dottie. And Lewis.

And Hugo.

There was nothing left to do here. Nothing at all. She gave her in-laws one last hug—one last smile—and then she crossed the graveyard and walked into the arms of her love.

CHAPTER ELEVEN

As WEDDINGS went, it was a pretty good wedding.

Toby knew about weddings. He knew the bride was supposed to look gorgeous. Well, Rachel looked gorgeous. Brides were supposed to be white and lacy and Rachel was lacy enough to be entirely satisfactory. Not too fussy, though, he decided. She had no veil or train. Her dress was made of white silk, Myra had told him. It was sort of bare around her shoulders with a floaty kind of skirt and bare feet. It was pretty nice, Toby decided—for a bride.

He wasn't sure about her feet, though. Bare toes. Weren't brides supposed to wear high heels? Still, that'd be pretty stupid on the beach where they'd decided to hold the ceremony. The ceremony was taking place on the exact spot where Rachel had taught him to drop-kick, the exact place where the townspeople had sheltered from the fire.

They were waiting for the ceremony to start. A couple of oldies from the nursing home were setting up a sound system. They were fiddling with knobs and Don was helping. It seemed like they were having a bit of trouble, but it didn't matter. Everyone was smiling and waiting, as though they had all the time in the world.

Which was fine for them, but Toby's football was up in the car. If he'd known he'd have to wait he could have brought it down for a quick kick.

He was a fantastic drop-kicker now. Rachel was all right at teaching him drop-kicking, he guessed—for a girl. She was better than his dad. But Lewis was... Well, Lewis was ace. He and Dottie, who refused to be called anything but

Lewis and Dottie, seemed to spend a heap of time here now. They loved Cowral. They loved Toby.

Which was fine by Toby. He loved Lewis and Dottie right back.

Life had expanded considerably for Toby.

Everyone he knew was on this beach. Such a crowd…

That was part of the reason they'd decided not to have the ceremony in Cowral's tiny church. There'd be people who wouldn't fit and who could miss out?

Myra was standing beside him. Toby was holding the ring and Myra was a bit worried that he'd drop it. As if he would.

Myra was looking a bit distracted, Toby thought, looking at her with affectionate appraisal. She'd spent the morning grooming the dogs to within an inch of their lives. Penelope looked gorgeous—well, she always did, though not quite so gorgeous now that Hugo and Rachel and Toby spent so much time on the beach. But Digger had come up respectably, too.

Knickers was here as well, with a great red bow round his neck— Knickers, the cocker spaniel, whose fight seemed to have started this whole chain of events. The black and white spaniel had recovered completely. So had Kim.

The girl was sitting hugging her knees on the sand as they waited for the ceremony to begin. Her dog was snuggled beside her. They looked great.

Pudge looked great, too, Toby conceded, moving on to the next dog in the pack of assorted canine guests. Pudge was still spending time with them, even though Sue-Ellen had returned. She'd been back in town for a few weeks now, staying in the hospital while her feet slowly healed. The townsfolk were rebuilding her cottage.

And one of the firefighters was with her. Gary. Toby had overheard Dad telling Rachel that maybe this was the best thing that could have happened to Sue-Ellen. Rachel said

Gary was big and kind and besotted. He'd carried Sue-Ellen out of the dam with her burnt feet, he'd visited her in Melbourne, he was pushing her wheelchair now and Rachel and Dad thought things were looking really interesting.

Dad said Gary even liked goats.

There were all sorts of interesting things happening in Cowral at the moment. Myra said the fire had started people thinking how transient life was—whatever that meant. Myra said it had something to do with being happy. Being happy now.

She said it also meant what was happening to Aunty Christine. She was here with that man. Michael.

Michael had come down one day soon after the fire to collect Penelope. He'd blustered in, really angry, saying there was no way Penelope could stay. And then he'd met Christine. Christine had been in their kitchen when he'd arrived. She'd been angry about Dottie and Rachel redecorating Toby's bedroom, so she'd been in the mood to yell, too. Anyway, Michael had yelled at Rachel, and Christine had yelled at Dad and then Michael and Christine had gone somewhere to complain some more and Rachel and Dad had grinned and Dad had said, 'Well, well, wonders will never cease.'

And it seemed Penelope could stay. Because of the mess at the dog show she hadn't got enough championship points to keep her place in the state's Afghan hound hierarchy, which meant Michael didn't want to breed from her—which was just fine by Rachel and Dad. Dad said any puppies of Penelope's would risk having a kangaroo loose in the top paddock and Rachel had giggled and agreed.

What was keeping them? They were taking so long. Gee, if there was just time to get his football…

But the oldies behind the sound system had finally suc-

ceeded. The sound system crackled into action and musi
blared out across the beach.

What was the song? Toby knew it. He knew it! It was
bouncing song! And everyone else in town knew it too
because in seconds the whole town was singing about grea
balls of fire at the top of their lungs.

Everyone was laughing as Rachel walked down the sand
beach. Lewis held her arm, as proud as any father, an
Dottie fussed over her dress, but it was Hugo Rachel wa
watching. Hugo who was waiting, with so much love in hi
eyes that even Toby could see it.

It was very satisfactory, Toby decided. He liked his da
looking like that. Soppy but good.

Then the tune ended and another started. Softer. Lovely

'It's Bach's ''Sheep May Softly Graze'',' Myra whis
pered, her eyes glistening with unshed tears. 'Becaus
they've come home to each other.'

Home. Here. Everyone was gazing at the shallows wher
once a township had sheltered to be safe and now a ma
and a woman were meeting each other, taking fingers i
hands and turning together to make these, the most sacre
of vows.

Toby even forgot his football.

> With this ring, I thee wed.
> With my body I thee worship.
> From this day forth.
> I now pronounce you…man and wife.

'I love you,' Hugo whispered, and Rachel looked into th
eyes of her second and most precious love and she whis
pered them back.

'I love you,' she whispered. 'Hugo McInnes, I love yo
for ever.'

*   *   *

Ace, thought Toby. It had gone off exactly as it should. Great vows! No one could wiggle out of this one.

Not that he thought they'd want to. Rachel and his dad were looking at each other with the goofiest grins. Matching grins. Any minute now… Yep, here it was. Yuck! The kiss.

If it had to be done, then it had to be done, he supposed. But he wished they'd get on with it.

There was football to be played. Wedding cake to be eaten.

Life to be lived.

Right now.

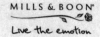

_MedicaL
romance™

THE ITALIAN SURGEON'S SECRET
by Margaret Barker

(Roman Hospital)

By leaving England to work in the A&E department of a Roman hospital Dr Lucy Montgomery hopes to focus on her career. But with handsome consultant Vittorio Vincenzi she discovers a bond that soon turns to desire. Vittorio wants to persuade Lucy to marry him, but he can't – not yet...

EMERGENCY MARRIAGE *by Olivia Gates*

Dr Laura Burnside was pregnant, single and alone. Her dream job had been snatched out of her hands by the arrogant Dr Armando Salazar, and she had nowhere to go. And then Armando made a proposal that turned her world upside down: marry him, give her child a father – and give in to the passion raging between them...

DR CHRISTIE'S BRIDE *by Leah Martyn*

Charming, handsome, a kind and talented doctor – Jude Christie seems the perfect man. And Dr Kellah Beaumont finds it impossible to resist when their growing attraction results in a passionate kiss. But as she comes to know Jude she realises that he has a secret standing in the way of their happiness...

On sale 3rd September 2004

FREE

4 BOOKS AND A SURPRISE GIFT!

We would like to take this opportunity to thank you for reading this Mills & Boon® book by offering you the chance to take FOUR more specially selected titles from the Medical Romance™ series absolutely FREE! We're also making this offer to introduce you to the benefits of the Reader Service™—

- ★ **FREE home delivery**
- ★ **FREE gifts and competitions**
- ★ **FREE monthly Newsletter**
- ★ **Books available before they're in the shops**
- ★ **Exclusive Reader Service offers**

Accepting these FREE books and gift places you under no obligation to buy; you may cancel at any time, even after receiving your free shipment. Simply complete your details below and return the entire page to the address below. You don't even need a stamp!

YES! Please send me 4 free Medical Romance books and a surprise gift. I understand that unless you hear from me, I will receive 6 superb new titles every month for just £2.69 each, postage and packing free. I am under no obligation to purchase any books and may cancel my subscription at any time. The free books and gift will be mine to keep in any case.

M4ZEE

Ms/Mrs/Miss/Mr..Initials ....
BLOCK CAPITALS PLEASE

Surname ....

Address ....

....

....Postcode ....

Send this whole page to:

The Reader Service, FREEPOST CN81, Croydon, CR9 3WZ